To Mom

*"You are here to be loved and to give love to those around you,
and nothing else really matters—it's that simple."*

Preface

Henry's Battalion began as a study exercise while I was serving as a missionary for the Church of Jesus Christ of Latter-Day Saints. I was curious to know more about angels and the kind of heavenly help we are privy to as children of God. One story that particularly inspired me was from the Old Testament—The prophet Elisha was caught in the middle of a war between Israel and Syria. While the Syrians bore down on the city he was in, his servant anxiously asked what they should do. Calmly, Elisha responded, "Fear not, for they that be with us are more than they that be with them." He prayed, and the Lord opened the eyes of his servant so that he could see that "the mountain was full of horses and chariots of fire round about Elisha" (2 Kings 6).

None of us suffer through exactly the same trials or weaknesses. We all have our own experiences on earth, and, hopefully, more often than not they are wonderful, happy ones—but they won't always. I used some of my experiences as a framework for Henry's Battalion, but I hope that anyone who reads this story will be able to put themselves and their own circumstances in place of mine and the fictional ones I came up with, and will know that they are never alone. God knows you. God loves you. We have to give this life everything we have, and still it will never be enough. But YOU are more enough. Because of that fact, we have a Savior, Jesus Christ, to make up the difference, and a Heavenly Father who loves us more than we could ever imagine, and behind them there are hosts of angels watching and protecting. Trials still come, tragedy still strikes, sorrow and agony are inescapable in this life. But we can *always* make it through, and become **better** and **stronger** and **more beautiful** because of it all. Sometimes you will have to fight for your joy and peace and happiness, but it is never gone or out of reach. Keep going.

"Be fixed in your purpose, for Satan will try you; the weight of your calling he perfectly knows. Your path may be thorny, but Jesus is nigh you; His arm is sufficient, tho demons oppose."

—LDS Hymnbook, 266 *The Time Is Far Spent*

Prologue

March 14, 1989

My sweet little Haley,

It has always been my belief that it is every child's unquestionable right to come into this world and expect her every physical need to be attended to. But more than that, she should be loved, cared for and cherished as a priceless treasure. Showing each other love is the reason why we are here on this earth—it is no chance coincidence or 'lucky' thing that just happens. So I want you to know that I love you beyond my ability to put into words. You should always know, no matter where you go, what you do or what happens to you in this tumultuous time, that you are indeed cherished—by me, by your father, and by your Heavenly Father and Mother. You are here to be loved and to give love to those around you, and nothing else really matters—it's that simple.

I guess first of all I want to tell you about your birth. After a long and miserable pregnancy, we planned your birth for the 9th of January (since we knew that you would be born by C-section. It seems that my body doesn't cooperate with labor, and we're both better off just bringing you out from the top). So I'm at my last doctor's appointment and good old Dr. Theurer teased me about showing up on the right day, as he knows how anxious I am (was). I teased him right back, because he actually forgot to show up in the delivery room for Paul's birth. (The OR personnel had to track him down while they threatened to let the janitor operate on me.) I said, "Now you're sure that you're not going to run off to the Bahamas and leave me to the janitor again, are you?" He looked at me with a totally blank stare and said, "By golly, I really am going to be in the Bahamas. I totally forgot." So we rescheduled your birthday for January 5th. Hope you like it. Dad and I had to be at the hospital at 6:00 am. They got me all ready to go. The anesthesiologist held a mirror for me so that I could see you be born. What an overwhelmingly awesome experience! First your little head and then your wet, squirming body. I have never felt closer to my Heavenly Father (and Mother), as you left one realm and entered another—mine! To hear your little cry and to know that you were healthy and beautiful still brings the tears. I would have loved you no matter how ugly or imperfect, but you weren't, you were gorgeous. The worth of such a gift could never be designated.

Our stay in the hospital was very peaceful and uneventful. It snowed and snowed, and I remember nursing you in the night with the lights off and watching the snowflakes glisten as they fell in the glow of the lights outside. I want your life to be just that secure, but I know that it won't be. You will have difficult, desperate times when you think that you are very alone in this world. You are not. You are of infinite worth and value and you have great potential. I know that, and your Father in Heaven knows that. My love and confidence will be with you always, as will His. Whatever you must endure—He understands. You can meet any challenge if you let Him be your friend. You can be a force for good in this world. At this point in my life, I think that the key to understanding the Savior is to be able to love and give when it is the most difficult. It's easy to love someone who loves you and is good to you, but can you truly love someone who you think is less deserving? I haven't conquered that yet, but I'm working on it.

You have been a wonderful nurser and a pretty good sleeper, in spite of these many weeks of colic. If we can lick that, we're in good shape. I will tell you lots more later but I need to go now. Love you infinity,

Mom

* * * * * * * * * * * * * * * *

June 3, 2012

Henry took in a deep breath before addressing his battalion. Every one of them was ready to follow him into this deepest of dark battles. At present they formed a protective circle around their captain and the shuddering figure kneeling on the ground next to him. Each of the half-dozen soldiers were on one knee, facing both their charge and their captain. Like a heavy fog, thick blackness swirled around them, surging and swelling as it poised itself to attack. With it came darting, smokey shadows even darker than the mass itself. Venomous hisses and insidious whispers escaped from it as it drew ever closer, smothering all other light and sound around it.

"Let no man's heart fail him—she needs us all tonight," Henry called to them. The determination and strength in his voice was accompanied by the slightest quiver, betraying his empathetic grief for the young woman huddled before him. "We all know how much the Opposition would love to topple a Great One, and we all know that she is tired, worn, and now a little broken." He knelt down next to the beloved soul entrusted to his guardianship. Reverently, he rested his strong hand on her shoulder. "But she has us, and we will not abandon her."

As he spoke, the noises issuing from the suffocating darkness grew more rabid and deranged. His battalion remained firm and undaunted, despite the sharp whispers of hatred and malice that cut through the air around them like serrated knives. Facing the imminent attack, each soldier stood resolute, eyes fixed on their captain, anticipating the coming target with iron fortitude and fiery courage. Angry demons lunged at the edges of the fog in a mad attempt to break free. It continued to converge on them, fueled by darkest doubts and twisted echoes of regret and anguish.

"Not to worry, Hal," said one of his soldiers, a young girl

who couldn't be older than twelve. She turned the baseball cap she
was wearing backwards. Her short, auburn hair framed her freckled,
smiling face. She twirled a slingshot in her hand and pulled a glowing,
golden ball out of a pouch at her waist and deftly loaded it into her
weapon. "We'll take care of them, you take care of her."

"That's my girl, Eden," Henry replied fondly. He turned to
an old, pleasant looking man wearing a sky blue bowtie and brown
suspenders over a plain, button-up shirt. "David, I'll leave it to you to
make the call. Tonight I think we needn't hold back."

"Yes sir, Captain," he replied with a smart salute. In his other
hand, supporting him as he knelt, was a wooden cane. The cracks in
the wood were filled with golden light, as if the core of the old walking
stick was made of the sun itself.

With a nod from Henry, the battalion stood and turned to
face the darkness, each of them wielding a weapon that glowed with
the same vibrant light as Eden's blazing marbles and David's cane.
Though few of them looked the part, they all had the stance and the
attitude of well-trained soldiers. Henry, grateful for his hearty troops,
watched as the darkness all but disappeared from within the circle.

Outside their formation, the wicked noise took on a frenzied,
ear-splitting volume. The edge of the black fog was tense, like a rubber
band being stretched tight. Suddenly, it broke, and out sprang a wild
horde of shadowy figures with a horrifying cry, something like the
terrorizing roar of a lion and the murderous scream of a raptor. Some
were like savage wolves, hunched over and running on all fours. Some
were almost the shape of humans, but for their snakelike faces and
strange, long limbs. Others were small and winged, and shrieked as

they flew through the fray, diving like hawks at their prey.

The face of every soldier was calm, though without a doubt they were fighting fiercely now. They wielded their weapons with destructive expertise to the dismay of the demons that bore down on them with frightening determination. Upon impact with the weapons, the creatures shrieked and burst like fireworks, only to be replaced by dozens more.

One guardian, a young woman with long, beautiful black hair and big, enchanting eyes took her place a few yards from Henry and began to sing. Her voice was soft and sweet, but full of resonant power that radiated from her in the form of golden light. Nearby, a girl even younger than Eden danced to the merry tune of the song, apparently oblivious to the ferocious battle surrounding her as she waved a long, golden ribbon through the air.

"Stephanie, sing the one about the tree!" she called to the singer. Stephanie smiled a wide, beautiful smile and gracefully changed her tune. The little girl moved about, spreading the light emanating from Stephanie with every sweeping twirl of her canary yellow sundress. Her tawny hair was messily braided, and the more she danced, the messier it became. Whenever one of the beasts got too close, she whipped out the ribbon, and the creature of the dark would explode with a howl upon contact.

"Got it!" she would yell triumphantly to Stephanie.

"Well done, Grace," Stephanie would reply with another angelic smile.

Henry, after watching the battle for a moment, did his best to ignore it and turned to the woman kneeling on the ground. His kindly face, bearing the gentle wrinkles of middle age, revealed a heart full of love and compassion as he knelt down in front of her, his knees touching hers.

"This isn't the end," he whispered, closing his hazel eyes and focusing his energy on the tiny, flickering light barely still alive in her core. "You are not alone."

The rest of the battalion continued to defend the circle as best they could despite the terrible onslaught of shifting, sharp shadows that had yet to cease pouring out of the fog.

The Opposition had found its prey in a most desperate moment, and was determined to make the most of it. The battalion, though some of its members had never faced such an attack, was unwilling to yield an inch. One soldier, a young man, was thrown to the ground by the charge of a particularly thick offender. He gave a furious yell, scooped up his sword and jumped to his feet. With one hard shake of the hilt of his sword and a soft but sharp *zing*, it became a bow instead. A full quiver appeared at his waist where his sword's sheath had been, and he fired the bright, golden arrows inside it with lightning speed. The quiver never emptied, and within a matter of seconds he had finished a dozen demons, each one swallowed up in the fiery light of the arrows that struck them. He could feel his heart race with the familiar rush of war. It wasn't exactly the same; as spirits, neither the guardians nor the demons could actually die. The demons, when they were defeated, were banished only temporarily. If a guardian was struck, the pain that was felt was more like a stab of anguish, a shot of sorrow—disorienting and debilitating blows of anxiety, confusion, frustration, or discouragement. They were precisely the wounds intended for the soul they were protecting.

"Dima!" Eden shouted in alarm. She was fighting with a dagger now. Her slingshot, less suitable for close combat, stuck out of her back pocket. The handsome young man turned and saw her pointing into the circle, where half a dozen demons now prowled, having snaked their way in during the brief moment that he was down. Dima nocked an arrow, drew back, and was about to release when one of the wolf-like creatures attacked from behind. It leapt onto his back and sent him once again sprawling; the arrow flew but missed it's target. Eden hurled the dagger at a monster running at her before grabbing her slingshot from her pocket. The sparks from the exploding enemy flew into her face. She waited a moment for her field of vision to clear, and then with absolute concentration and practiced aim, let loose one of the golden marbles from her pouch. It struck the snarling creature directly in the head and the beast burst into shards of light, freeing Dima. She grabbed her dagger and ran to his side, where David had already appeared. Back to back the three of them fought the whole pack of devil wolves that had arrived from out of the fog to replace the fallen one. David handled his cane like a sword, and with deftness and agility uncommon for his age he did battle like the fiercest of warriors. He flipped the cane over and used the crook to pull one of the creatures off of Eden, then sharply flung the beast away. In the same swing he took out a couple of the hawk-like demons, just before they could finish their dive towards Dima. Despite the trio's impressive skill, and that of the rest of the battalion, there seemed to be little progress made.

Henry, who had taken his attention momentarily off of his charge to assess the state of his battalion, saw several dark monsters

now circling in towards him, closer and closer. He stood and
unsheathed his own sword in one swift movement. Though he looked
like a simple, quiet man, and the plain clothes he wore suggested a past
full of common labor, his blade sliced through the heartless hellions
with the skill and ease of a seasoned warrior as they suddenly attacked
from every direction. The Darkness may have been determined, but
Henry was defending someone he loved. They stood no chance against
him. As the last demon in the pack fell to his sword with a furious hiss
and a burst of garish light, he heard Dima shouting.

"This isn't working!" he said. His bow was now a battle axe.

"Form ranks!" David called, barely heard over the din of the
demonic Opposition.

In the course of the battle, their circle formation had become
scattered. At David's call, each of them simultaneously sheathed or
stowed their weapons. Grace tied her ribbon in her hair. Dima gave
his axe a shake and it became a simple iron rod which he tucked into
his belt. David rested his cane in the crook of his arm. They were all
back in the circle in less than a moment, standing about three or four
feet apart. The battalion seemed to collectively inhale before they
reverently stretched their arms out towards each other, palms facing
upward, and closed their eyes.

"Send us more Light," David said, his tone prayerful.

In between each of them appeared a being made entirely of
light. Shaped like humans, these shining beings linked hands with the
guardians, doubling their force. Almost immediately, from the heart of
every member of the battalion, a faint golden light began to emanate—
small at first but growing ever brighter. Soon, it was almost blinding.

The magnificent and unconstrained energy they could now produce with the help of the new Light required the unbridled strength and absolute focus of every guardian.

Henry inhaled deeply and exhaled softly, kneeling down again next to the sorrowing soul. He put his forehead to hers, wrapped his strong hands around her prayerful ones, and pinched his eyes shut. He softly hummed the tune of her favorite hymn, and as he did so, he too began to emanate a warm, gentle light.

A particularly heinous creature of the Darkness dug its long, crooked claws into the ground, withstanding the force of the light that had begun to blow away the other creatures like a powerful wind. Over the shoulder of the Great One he protected, Henry saw the loathsome thing, the size of a grizzly bear, crouching just outside the circle. It seemed to be trembling under the effort to stay and advance, its hunched and undefined form wavering in the light. Its wicked eyes were fixed on Henry, who remained unflinching under the scathing glare. Henry ignored the sickening snarls and snapping, drooling jowls and focused his attention wholly on the soul before him. Her hands were clasped tightly in prayer—so tightly that her knuckles were white from the strain. Her head was bowed, in reverence as well as in anguished despair. Her whispered communion with Deity was accentuated with tears and quiet, shuddering sobs.

The maniacal creature peered through the ring of guardians and light beings, whose attention was consumed by the effort to sustain the growing light. It took several running dashes at the young woman, jumping between the unmoving sentinels. Henry's light originated in his core, near his heart, but with each attack it exploded out in every direction and struck the beast like the blast from a bomb, sending the miserable thing sprawling. The beast became more agitated and angry with every failed attempt. Finally, in a crazed and enraged fit, it dove at the woman, the intention to tear her to pieces evident on its snarling, ugly face. Henry bowed his head, and with a burst of light brighter than the rest, he banished the persistent fiend from the light into which it had trespassed.

Henry took several slow, deep breaths. Stephanie took up the tune of the song he had been humming, and soon the whole battalion lended their voices. After what could have been minutes or what could have been hours, the darkness and its depraved minions were entirely overcome by the light of the little battalion, which, in the end, shined as bright as midday sun. The tears on the face of the prayerful one dried, her shuddering ceased, and a small light kindled again in her soul and could faintly be seen by all around. Henry opened his eyes and leaned back from her. He gave a great sigh of relief.

"Resilient as ever," he said softly with a quiet smile. He stood and looked around him. The sun was just breaking the horizon, and its fresh light made the dew on the grass sparkle cheerfully. A kindly breeze rustled the row of towering cottonwood trees nearby, and birds sang brightly to gently wake up their world. The glowing newcomers seemed to bow their heads reverently to the battalion before dissolving into the dazzling morning light. The guardians let their hands fall back to their sides, their shoulders relaxing and their smiles returning.

"Piece of cake," said Eden as she spun her hat back to the front.

"For us, maybe," responded the gentlemanly David. He didn't seem like much of a warrior with his slight form and wavy grey hair, bow tie and loafers, but he was in fact one of the strongest of the guardians. "Not such an easy task for Haley." He sighed and shook his head. "We all knew it was coming. She did too, in a way. Doesn't matter how much you know, still hurts."

Henry nodded.

"Eden?"

"Yes, Hal?" she replied eagerly, anxious for an assignment.

"Come here and stay right by her, alright?"

Eden instantly obliged.

"Don't you worry about a thing. I'll take good care of her," she said, clearly pleased to be entrusted with such a duty. Henry couldn't help but crack a little smile and shake his head.

"A hundred years in the service and you think you know it all," he said.

"Hey, that's a hundred and six to you, sir, and I am a fast learner. Gabriel himself said so."

"She'll be the captain of her own battalion before long," chuckled David, who stood nearby, leaning on his cane.

With a grin and a wink, Henry disappeared.

One

I lay on the porch swing where I had fallen asleep the night
before. I could feel the sunlight warming my face through the
branches of the apricot trees and the wind swaying my makeshift bed.
Somewhere between sleep and wakefulness, I heard a young voice
whisper.

"I think she's waking up now!"

Another voice, this one just as gentle but quite a bit gruffer and
much older, responded.

"We should let her be."

"Oh, but I would so love to speak to her!" implored the young
one.

"Come now, let her sleep. She needs her rest," answered the
other.

"I promised I would stay right by her side," said the little one. "I won't leave her."

I felt something soft, like the fingers of a child, touch my open palm. As I went to close my hand around them, a door inside the house slammed shut, and I came into full consciousness. The voices, the small hand, and the comfort of the invisible, perhaps dreamed company disappeared. With my eyes still firmly shut, I desperately tried to pull them back to me, but they were gone. The porch door nearby opened with a grating screech, and a shadow fell over me.

"We're gonna be late," my sister said. With great effort, I opened one eye to look at her. Her blonde hair was remarkably neat. She generally resorted to ponytails and braids, but today it was down and fell over her shoulders in gentle, golden waves. She wore a simple green dress and a light, white cardigan. Her hazel eyes were brave, but I could see the tension in her jaw holding back her emotions. She'd been like that ever since I got home the night before last.

I sighed and sat up, then patted the swing next to me. She hesitated a moment, then came and sat down. She stared into the space in front of us. The yard was big—two acres in all. There, past the apricot trees and behind the cottonwoods, stood two abandoned playhouses from our childhood. Abandoned, that is, unless you count the spiders, potato bugs, and earwigs. One was purple, the other was white and up on stilts. You had to climb up a bee-infested ladder made of three old tires stacked end-on-end, or shimmy up the rusty fire pole, to get up to the small platform protected by a deteriorating roof. Next to that was a huge sandbox—also known as the world's biggest litter box thanks to the half-dozen cats that ignored us humans but loved our property. I'm sure they thought they were wild, and they almost were. Besides the stinky little presents left by the cats, there were hundreds and hundreds of tiny sea shells. Mom used to bring them home in milk jugs, who knows from where, and spread them out in the sand so we could search for them. We had the better part of two decades to find them, but there were still plenty left behind.

Beyond that was the spacious garden, filled mostly with weeds now. Once, it had been filled with far more bountiful plants. How frustrated I had been as a child to be woken up every morning in the summer before the sun had even crept over the mountains to pull weeds, water, and obey the instructions of Mom, the master gardener. As the season progressed, we had fresh tomatoes, carrots, peas, corn, peaches, raspberries, squash, and so many other delights to choose from; my complaining didn't cease but my young soul did rejoice.

Near the garden was the chicken coop, empty now. I could remember many Saturdays being spent shoveling out the wood shavings mingled with chicken poop so that Dad could haul in the fresh stuff. As bad as it had smelled before, the clean bedding was reminiscent of our frequent camping trips to the nearby forested mountains.

Collecting eggs, on the other hand, had been a daily job—and a dangerous one, too, or so it felt when I was a kid. Some of those hens were fierce, and that dang rooster...well, let's just say my brother never did get over his fear of roosters.

Further on was the pasture and the barn. It was more or less a jungle back there, since it had been a year or two since any cow or goat or horse had roamed and grazed. It was a grasshopper heaven.

The giant weeds jerked and swayed as the champion jumpers lived the insect dream. The barn was sky blue instead of the typical red, and had two stalls, a loft, and an area for tack, hay, and tools. Climbing in those rafters, ironically, had seemed less dangerous than gathering chicken eggs, despite the twenty-foot drop to the stalls below.

In front of us were the apricot trees. Tiny, baby green apricots were beginning to form on the dark, twisted branches. Apricot jam was a particularly delicious prize that came at the expense of the particularly hated task of picking up the rotten ones that had fallen on the grass below so that the lawn mower didn't hit the rock-like pits.

But she wasn't looking at any of that. Not really.

"Your hair's cute," I said.

"Thanks. I showered," she responded flatly. I gave a low whistle to show how impressed I was.

"Wow."

She finally looked at me, and despite ourselves, we laughed. Just for a second or two, but we laughed. Showers generally weren't a priority. Not for Suzy. We went in the house together, she helped me with my hair, I put on my blue dress, and we left. As we drove down the long driveway, over the bridge with the creek running under it, I scowled at the dozens of new houses and roads that filled what had once been farmland and encroached on our little paradise. Maybe it was better this part of life was coming to an end.

* * * * * * * * * * * * * * *

So many tears, some smiles, soft voices, hugs and kisses—I felt like I was drowning in it all. One after another they came. I knew some of them, though many of them were strangers or nearly so. Maybe I had seen them once or twice, or they knew me when I was a baby. I couldn't say. I felt split—part of me was raging like the wildest of hurricanes with grief and anger, the other part was still and calm, like dawn in a mountain meadow. Part of me was relieved to be there, part of me wished I was still far, far away. I'm not sure how the different versions of myself coincided in my body, but somehow they did, and somehow I kept standing there, next to the casket, next to my sister and my brother.

My mind drifted as I stood, shaking some hands, smiling, nodding, even giving the occasional hug, always reverently folding my hands in between. I was genuinely grateful for the show of love and support but nonetheless irritated by it. A week ago everything was normal; Suzy was in high school, Paul, my older brother, was slaving away at his corporate job, Mom was working part time, Dad and his wife, Lila, were building a new house, and I was away again. This time I was teaching English in a small village in Ukraine. Before that, China. Before that, working at a lodge in Alaska. Before that, exploring California. It had been over a year since I'd been home.

It wasn't easy in Ukraine. It was a boarding school, and the kids I was teaching were difficult. I bonded with some, but others just refused to accept me and constantly made my class a misery. The last time I had spoken with my mom was Mother's Day. We had done a video chat on the computer. It took ages to get it working, even though we'd done it a dozen times before. She wasn't exactly technologically inclined, and the internet at the school was infuriatingly finicky. I tried to be brave. I told her things were okay, they were tough, but okay. I was happy, I lied. She knew I was lying. She said she was proud of me for helping others, but that I mustn't forget to help myself as well. She didn't look so well. She was pale, and the light in her eyes was faded and weak. I was too wrapped up in my own troubles to really notice, though. I only realized it later. Too much later. When we were finished talking, I felt better—ready to give teaching those little menaces another go.

Then, a few days ago, the call came. She was gone, just like that. No one could tell me what happened, just that she was gone. I called my brother, my dad, my best friend, no one knew what exactly happened, what caused it. I threw the few belongings I had with me into my suitcase and left the school. At the airport they told me I would have to pay to check my bag. Fifteen dollars per kilo. I tried to explain that there had to be some mix up, I hadn't had to pay that much for luggage before, but I didn't know any Russian or Ukrainian and their English was dismal. Who works at an international airport and doesn't speak English? Come on. My blood boiled and my head fogged and I thought I might quite literally explode. My chest felt like it was rapidly expanding and pretty soon my skin wouldn't be able to hold me together any more. I didn't have money, I was volunteering and had paid my last penny five minutes before to get my plane ticket home.

"Forget it!" I had shouted, and stalked off with my suitcase in tow. The airport staff and all the passengers nearby watched as I tossed the suitcase and everything inside—souvenirs, clothes, books—into a dumpster just outside the doors. I stormed back and put on the kindest, calmest smile I could and said coldly, "May I please board the plane now?"

A layover in Paris, a layover in Dallas, all in all it was about twenty-four hours of time by myself to think about what had happened. I thought mostly about Suzy. She had been the one to find her. I heard the story mostly from others, a little bit from her. It was her last day of high school—yearbook day. She had been staying at our dad's house that week, but came by that morning. I wasn't there. I wish I had been. I was on the other side of the globe, trying to do some good in the world, or so I told myself. Trying to escape real life and responsibility was more like it. When I called her after I'd heard what happened, she didn't say much. She said she was okay. Lying about how we feel is sort of a family vice. I can only imagine what it must have felt like to come home thinking everything was like it always was, only to have your entire world shattered to pieces right in front of your eyes.

She had stopped by after a sleepover on the softball diamond with her team to pick something up before heading to the school to sign yearbooks. Immediately she realized that Mom wasn't where she usually was, in that horrible, broken recliner where she slept every night. The lamp on the little table next to the recliner was still on, and the tv was a static screen. Even when she saw her, lying on the floor next to the computer in the other room, it didn't register. She bustled about, saying, "Mom," over and over again, almost annoyed, thinking she had fallen asleep there on her meds. "Mom, Mom, MOM!" she said as she put her bag down in the kitchen. When Mom was on her meds, it was always like this. Then she noticed Jake, the neurotic border collie lab mix that owed his life to my mom—all of us had imagined up clever ways to off that nuisance. He had chewed up hundreds if not thousands of dollars worth of furniture, pillows, toys, books—you name it—as he transitioned from an abusive home to her loving one. When Suzy realized Jake was huddled under the computer table, acting "psycho" and licking Mom's hand, her heart must have sunk to the core of the earth. Annoyance turned dramatically to devastation and panic upon realizing that something was horribly, horribly wrong.

I shook myself back to reality after another funeral guest said hello to me for the second time. I hadn't heard him at first. I smiled politely, nodded and said, "Oh how nice," when he told me how he knew my mom from her days as an ER nurse. He moved on to Suzy and Paul.

I thought of the first funeral I had ever attended. I was nine years old. My oldest cousin had been in a car accident, and for eleven days we waited and waited while she was on life support, wondering and hoping and praying. Her heart kept beating, but the doctors eventually told her parents that she wasn't going to wake up again. At her funeral, my grandma passed each of us granddaughters a handkerchief, and my youngest aunt, who had been closest to Stephanie, followed behind her and snatched each one of them back because, she said, she was going to need all of them. I remember how pale she was, lying in her casket. I remember wishing she didn't have to go—she was so nice, and she had the most beautiful smile I had ever seen. I remember feeling sorry that I wished she wasn't gone, thinking that she must be so happy where she is now, with Heavenly

Father, why wouldn't she be? My nine-year-old self had been much more accepting of death than my adult self.

Another smile and a kind, encouraging squeeze of my hand from a stranger, and my mind drifted back again. I tried to listen to the things people were saying to me, I tried to accept their condolences, their advice, their well-wishes, but none of it sank in, none of it really even made it all the way to my brain before I discarded it. Back into the depths and security of my mind I went.

Suzy, Paul, and Paul's wife, Amelia, had picked me up from the airport and immediately began discussing the funeral. It was in a day and a half, and they wanted me to do the life sketch and sing a song. I'd been gone almost a year, but there was no time for acclimating to home or catching up. We had to plan and arrange and decide and facilitate—there was no time. I felt numb all the way up until the viewing the night before. That's when I first started to feel irritated by the sentiments of those wanting to grieve with us. It wasn't fair, it wasn't kind, but I just didn't want to be smothered by their feelings, I wanted to deal with my own. I reminded myself over and over again that this wasn't about me, it was about Mom, and these were her friends, and our family, and they loved her, too. And they loved me and my siblings. They were there to support us, to care for us. And yet...I was still irritated.

Last night, after the viewing, we pulled down the long driveway to Mom's house. Paul put the car into park and I jumped out and stormed off into the night. I glared at the cheerful leaves on the apricot trees, shimmering in the moonlight. I ignored the daffodils and the tulips bouncing their lovely heads in the gentle, cool breeze. I gritted my teeth and cursed the lilac bush, towering over my head and wrapping me up in its heavenly scent, kindly inviting me to relax on the old bench beneath it. I collapsed on the grass near the garden and cried and cried, for the first time since hearing the news. I cried before, but I hadn't yet absorbed what was happening. When we pulled up to her house that night, and she wasn't there because we'd left her back at the mortuary, I was through. I was done. I wanted no more of this nonsense, I wanted things to go back to the way they were, I wanted to see her again, I wanted my mom. The grass was soft and sweet, my tears were bitter and angry.

My hands clenched together in prayer. Not really the faithful, humble kind of prayer. Not at first, at least. More the confused, desperate kind. I didn't really pray in words, just feelings. I felt like all the light was draining from the world and I couldn't do anything to keep it here. Why was this happening? I wasn't ready, I wasn't prepared, I hadn't agreed to this. I didn't want this. This anger was a new emotion for me. At least, one I had never really allowed myself to fully experience. Since the time I had learned I could control my emotions, I had snuffed this particular one out before it was barely more than a spark. For the first time, it was a raging wildfire, and it felt good. Cleansing, almost, in its fury. At the same time, however, I could feel every speck of my soul being severely scorched.

Slowly, as I continued to pour out my feelings in that messy, tearful prayer, things started to change. I don't know just how long I was there on the grass, but as the time passed, the darkness didn't seem so loud, and the light seemed to fight for its place. I don't know how the turmoil in my soul changed to peace, but somehow it did, and I awoke the next morning on the porch swing with sweet voices in my head and warm, nurturing sunlight on my face.

Now I was here, at my mother's funeral. Peace and turmoil battled inside me once more, but overall I managed to stay calm. Those that spoke shared things about her that I never knew or didn't realize. I got to know her a little better. I looked at my tiny nephew in Amelia's arms, sitting down the bench from me, and realized I wasn't the only one missing out here. I kept thinking about those voices I had heard that morning, that child that had vowed to stay by my side...I could have sworn I was actually hearing her voice, and the other voice, too...they were familiar, but I couldn't place them. And the hand that had touched mine...I had actually felt that. Yet all of it was gone in a flash. A dream, I supposed. A lovely, comforting dream. Those voices had seemed like they could calm every storm that raged in my heart. But they weren't real. Just a dream.

Two

Henry sat on a porch swing that creaked threateningly, due only to the almost imperceptible breeze. Had he actually had any mass, it would have collapsed under his weight immediately, and not just the swing, but the entire porch as well. Being a spirit without a body had its benefits. Next to him, as weightless as its owner, was the golden sword he had used the night before to defend Haley. It was a simple weapon, but issued a celestial light, like morning sunshine.

The small cabin that the porch was attached to sat near a bend in the river, and looked a bit like a skeleton. It was tired and leaning. All of the windows had long since broken; wisps of what had once been curtains clung to their frames. In some places, the logs, softened by time and weather, had started crumbling back to the earth. Spiders, termites and other crawlers enjoyed the food and the homes it provided. Grass and weeds had grown up all around and even on the little dwelling. It was almost entirely swallowed up by the forest.

All around him, life bustled about. A rufous hummingbird buzzed happily from flower to flower. An acorn woodpecker drilled away at a nearby lodgepole pine, long since dead, filling its newly dug pockets with acorns and chasing away a pesky Stellar's jay that was bent on stealing his hard-earned stores. A chattering squirrel chased a happy pair of mountain chickadees out of his tree, below which a doe and her little fawn meandered as they grazed contentedly. A gray fox was curled up on the porch a few feet from where Henry sat, snoozing peacefully despite the raucous noise coming from two boisterous chipmunks playing chase on the dilapidated roof. Even a large mama black bear ambled through the clearing with her two cubs, happily picking away at the blackberry bush that had taken over much of what had once been a lovely garden patch. Henry loved the creatures of the woods. In his life, he had learned their names and habits, and they had become his friends. After the loss of his wife and baby boy, he found human interaction painful and difficult. The animals had been much more comforting and understanding. Although this was a generation of critters far removed from the ones he had known so well, they seemed to sense his presence and gathered to keep him company as he took a short respite from his labors.

A moment later, a kind looking woman appeared on the swing next to him. Far from being startled, Henry felt a wave of relief come over him.

"Please tell me you are here to take my job," he said. She smiled warmly.

"No, I'm afraid not. I had my turn already," she responded,

adjusting the hem of her plaid, blue-and-red button-up shirt. Then, with a wry smile, she added, "She isn't giving you too much trouble, is she? She doesn't look it, but she's fiery."

"Gracious, no. Not her. But someone has it in for her, that's for sure."

The newcomer nodded, her brown eyes squinting a little with concern. "Someone has it in for all of us, if you ask me. But yes...her especially."

Henry sighed heavily. "Frankly, I don't feel very qualified for this job. Sometimes, when we're fighting, I feel sad for the ones attacking us. There must be some real sorrow in them to kindle such rage. When the battle's done and she still feels destroyed, it's like nobody won. I just wish I could do more. If I could somehow help her to see..." He sighed again.

"Well," said the woman with another kind smile, "I think your empathy gives you great strength. And you know what they say—seeing is believing. But then, if we could see everything, know everything, what would be the point of faith? What would we learn?" She grinned as the fox stretched and yawned a bit overdramatically. "I mean it when I say she's fiery. Her soul is *made* of fire. It used to give her so much light and warmth, but I think now she only lets it burn her. It's part of her that she doesn't know anymore—she thinks it's something separate, something bad that she has to put down and get rid of. She's fighting a double battle, against the Opposition and against herself. Your job isn't an easy one, Captain. But, I know she is in wonderful hands. I'll be around if you need me. The assignment I was given allows me plenty of flexibility. Henry," she said, meaningfully, "thank you."

And with that, she was gone. The chipmunks, who seemed to have stopped their game of chase to catch their breath and eavesdrop, started up again, and the woodpecker, remembering his annoyance, squawked once more at the jay. Henry wished he could stay there forever. He wished he had more memories of this place, memories with his family. A twinge of guilt pricked him as he quietly pined for what might have been. He knew the promise had been made, the price had been paid, for his happiness. Nothing, not even the unexpected, almost unbearable twists and turns of mortality, could keep him from that. Still, some days waiting was hard.

Gathering his strength and his courage, Henry was about to depart as well when another visitor silently and suddenly, with just the softest flash of light, appeared next to him on the swing. Henry sat back again and smiled wearily.

"Just a quick break, Gabriel. I was on my way back now."

"Oh, I'm not here to scold you, my friend," smiled the noble and ever-patient Gabriel. "It's a misconception that spirits don't get tired—certainly not physically tired, but your work is difficult and I won't blame you for needing a moment." He paused, still smiling. "This is a lovely home."

Henry looked around him with a nostalgic, somewhat melancholy nod. "It would have been."

"No, no, it was. And is. I know it didn't get the kind of use you had hoped for," he said, eyeing an old wooden swing hanging from a nearby sycamore tree. The moss-covered rope had given out on one side, and the seat hung sadly from the other. "Still, it is lovely.

Many moments that seem lost are only postponed, you know." The chickadees fluttered right past them as if to say hello.

Henry pondered his words, and as he gazed up into the sunlit canopy, he seemed to decide that his companion was right. His regret ebbed, and then flowed back to his previous uneasy thoughts.

"I'm not sure I'm doing a very good job," Henry suddenly blurted, as if the admission was one he had been trying to hold back but couldn't any longer. Gabriel smiled gently.

"What makes you say that? I heard all about your bout with the Opposition the other night. Sounds to me like you are the perfect man for this position."

"Gabriel, I am a *simple* man," Henry exclaimed, throwing his hands up. "I should be assigned to a simple soul. She's a Great One, for Heaven's sake!"

"Oh, I think Heaven knows full well who she is. And who you are, for that matter. I'm not sure I understand what you are referring to...a simple soul? I'm quite certain there is no such thing." Henry didn't look encouraged. "Look, dear man, I understand how overwhelmed and underqualified you must feel. There are few of us who feel up to the tasks we are given, but they are ours to fulfill, so...we do them. Like I say, Heaven knows full well who she is. It's part of the test, however, that she doesn't have the full extent of that knowledge. *I* know exactly who she is, Henry. She fought by my side in the War, just as she did by yours. You have a whole battalion at your disposal, and even more help than that, whenever you need it. You aren't in this alone. None of us are."

"You know, the Living have this idea that death is a state of 'rest.' I've never worked so hard in my life."

Gabriel chuckled, and his eyes, at once ageless and ancient, were crinkled by wrinkles that bore witness of the numberless smiles that had crossed his face.

"A bit like a cruel joke, isn't it?" His smile faded somewhat as his eyes grew more serious. "This work, Henry, is the greatest work we can do. There is a Plan for all of us, a purpose for which we are all striving. We can't do it alone. You had your own battalion watching over you, and they wept for your sorrows and fought for your soul." In his hands now was the golden sword. He handed it to Henry, who took it reverently.

"The captain of my battalion gave this to me," he said softly, gripping the hilt firmly. It was a very simple, long sword called a Roman spatha. The rounded, wooden pommel was followed by a simple handle, a small guard, and a plain blade. If it weren't for the light that came from it, it wouldn't be much to look at. "She said it only seemed right that it should keep fighting for me."

"Ah, yes, I know that sword. It has defended some of the greatest souls I've ever known, though no one would have heard of them." Gabriel paused, then smiled and put a hand on Henry's shoulder. "Struggling is what makes us great. Look at this river," he said, nodding towards it. "It chooses the path of least resistance. It chooses not to struggle, and yes, it seems to have quite the peaceful existence. But look how crooked it is. To be strong and straight is difficult. Sometimes the path you take must be the path of *most* resistance." He took a breath and looked at his companion. "But you already know that. And you know that Heaven has already qualified you for every task, for every opponent, that you meet."

There was a brief moment of silence between them, interrupted by the two bear cubs wrestling noisily nearby. Henry smiled, exhaling slowly.

"I will go and do," he said, a bit wearily, but with sincerity.

Gabriel matched his smile, and stood up, facing the river.

"When they first come to Earth, you can see it in their eyes that they still know, at least faintly, who they are. It would make our jobs so easy if even for a small moment they could remember just enough of their worth, of their absolute brilliance, to defy all Opposition. But that is not the Plan. And that is why Haley has you. It is your job to help her remember. Remember how her face had shone with conviction, with courage, with absolute certainty of her divine heritage? Remember how the Opposition had cowered before her?" Henry was nodding. "She won't remember those things, not yet. But she can remember the way she felt, especially the way she felt about herself. She can learn to love herself the way we do, the way He does. Then her greatness will be free to spread to others."

Henry's heart suddenly swelled with new courage and strength of its own. He stood with such purpose, such determination, that all of the animals in the meadow stopped what they were doing and looked his way. Without another word, he sheathed his sword and vanished.

Gabriel sighed contentedly. He bent down to the fox, which had got to its feet, stretched lazily, and wandered over to sit next to the Archangel. He scratched its head, and it leaned into him like it could feel the gesture.

"There's work to do," he said warmly, his eyes twinkling with an affectionate smile. He, too, vanished.

* * * * * * * * * * * * * * * *

November 20, 1991

Sweet Haley,

I really don't have time to write this morning, but I couldn't pass this magical moment by. It is the morning of the first snowfall of the year. Paul has just caught the bus to school and Suzy is in her highchair eating Cheerios. You have dressed up your almost-three-year-old self in mis-matched snow clothes and you are outside exploring. I am watching you through the window as you go to each tree branch and inspect the clinging fluffs before you brush them off. Then you taste a handful and trudge off to check out something else. The big dogs are frolicking around you, and they shepherd you from one part of the yard to the next. I am sure that there have been many first snowfalls for millions of children throughout time. But the wonder and joy on your little face makes my soul smile and gives me shivers. It is one of those re-affirmations of life. I am truly grateful every day to be your mother. I could not be happier or feel more blessed. Love you infinity,

Mom

Three

I remember riding in the limo from the mortuary to the
cemetery with Suzy, Paul, Amelia and baby Charlie, who I had met for
the first time in person just a couple days before. He was so little, and
so blissfully unaware of the turmoil. While all of our worlds seemed
to be collapsing in on themselves, his miraculously stood unscathed. I
envied him, wishing I could be the one snugly strapped into a car seat,
sleeping away the horrible day.

As we drove through the neighborhoods to the final resting
place of our mother, Paul remarked on how strange it was to see
everyone else going about their business like it was a normal day. We
watched them from the windows as they mowed their lawns, played
in sprinklers, loaded up their cars with picnics, ran errands, walked
their dogs...I didn't think it was strange. I thought it was rude, and I
was angry. It was a muffled, muted kind of anger. My hands didn't

tremble and my brain didn't fog like it did with the anger I had felt the night before. No, this was more of a smouldering, sizzling bitterness that just made me feel tired and sweaty. Something at the back of my conscience tried to remind me of the peaceful, sweet feeling I had had when I awoke that morning, but something else in me quickly and stubbornly smothered it. When I was younger and my family had faced divorce, I had resiliently pledged myself to positivity and cheerfulness. It had worked, for the most part. I was known as a happy, strong person and commended for it. I always had useful, uplifting things to say, and a pleasant hope for the future. Well, it wasn't working this time. Something in me was broken, and I wasn't feeling very positive or strong anymore.

But, despite my resentment, the world did go on. Days did become like normal days again. Eventually. For a long time after, there was so much to sort out—the bank, the credit card companies, subscriptions, the mortgage, the phone company—over and over again having to explain to strangers that we had just unexpectedly lost our mother, and so they should no longer expect any payments, please and thank you. I only made a few calls. Paul, being the oldest, and having a house and a family and a full time job, knew things about the world that Suzy and I didn't. He knew all of the things that needed to be done to pry our family from the jaws of Mom's creditors and commitments. And he did it. I don't know how he managed. I guess in times like those, you just buckle up and get things done even when you are certain you have reached the very edge of your endurance. I clung to that edge with just my fingertips, and I think Paul knew it. He stepped up and took care of it. He didn't ask much of us, and I was so thankful.

One of the few things he did ask for my help with had been to call the phone company. It didn't seem too complicated, so I accepted, anxious to do something helpful. They answered, and I explained.

"Hi...uh...so I'm just calling because I need to cancel my mom's cell phone service. She passed away last week, so...we don't need it anymore..."

"Sorry for your loss, let me transfer you."

"May I help you?"

"Yeah, hi. I just need to cancel my mom's cell service. She... she, uh, passed away unexpectedly last week, so..."

"Oh, so sorry for your loss. I'm going to need to transfer you."

There were desperate tears streaming down my face that felt like they were boiling with my frustration, sorrow, and fury long before I could explain, for the third time, why I had called, let alone actually accomplish anything with the customer service representative. It was like I had finally divulged a horrible secret I was trying to hold as tightly to my person as I could, but now it was out, and like the windborne seeds of a dandelion, it would spread in every direction and surely everyone would know. She was gone.

It took the entire summer to clean out the house. Paul took a practical approach. If none of us could use it, and it's sentimental value wasn't great, it was gone. We hauled away loads and loads of stuff. Just stuff. Suzy and I, being more transient, didn't really know what to say. Did I want a toaster? Could Suzy use a vacuum cleaner? Then there were the clothes. Some were easy, but some...that blouse she always wore, or that jacket she loved, or that dress that she looked so bright and happy in, even that t-shirt we all hated...for some reason, throwing them out felt a bit like losing her all over again.

Some days were fine, even fun—there is something liberating about getting rid of junk. Some days were desperately difficult. Some days were just...days. Numb, ugly days.

On one day, somewhere between desperately difficult and numb, we chanced upon something that changed things for me—for all of us. We were sorting through more stuff...had it belonged to a grandmother, or come from a supermarket? Was it valuable, or hardly worth bothering with? Was it mine? Suzy's? Paul's? Gosh it was tedious. We came to a large, ceramic pitcher residing in a large, ceramic bowl. No one had any idea where it came from. It was all wrapped up in bubble wrap, it must have had some value, yet it had been stuffed in the deepest corner of the closet. Antique? No idea. After a few moments of deliberation, we all voted it was fit for Goodwill. Into the pile it went. I don't remember which one of us hesitated a few moments later and decided it was worth unwrapping and taking a closer look, but I will be forever grateful that we did. Tucked inside was a scrap of paper, and written on that piece of paper were words that later sustained me when I thought surely I'd crumple up and disappear. It was folded into quarters, and had other notes and a child's scribbles all over it. The title, written neatly across the top and underlined, was *10 Most Important Things That I Want My Children to Know and Learn,* with her name written in small letters next to it. And then followed the list:

1. Heavenly Father loves you and knows the intimate details of your life.

2. Becoming a disciple of Christ enhances the quality of your life in every way, diminishes nothing.

3. Truly, if you have done it unto the least of your brethren, you have done it unto Him.

4. The Gospel laws are present and in effect whether you choose to acknowledge them or not.

5. Life is not fair. Sometimes people are not fair, but those two facts do not change who you are and what you know about eternal truths.

6. People are so much more important than jobs, meetings, projects, deadlines, etc...

7. Right behind the essential qualities of kindness and selflessness and a loving heart are honesty, integrity, purity, and humility.

8. This one should have been after #1. That is: talk to and listen to that Father who loves you so much and so well.

9. We are ingrained from birth with an aversion to and avoidance of death. But it is only the loneliness and the longing of being left behind that is difficult. Death is actually an advancement, a joyous promotion, which if we could, we should celebrate. Live each day with those you love as if it were your last together. Let there be no regrets, no unfinished business. And yet remember that the great principle of forgiveness exists. There will be time beyond the grave to finish all business, but peace and happiness can be yours whenever you want it enough.

10. As your earthly parent, I want you to know how very much I love you. I loved you before you were even born, and wanted you and anticipated your arrival with great joy and longing. I am grateful that you chose to accept me as your mother, and I am happy for every moment that we have been together, and for the eternity that we have to continue in our love.

At first my heart struggled between relief, gratitude, and that lingering awful bitterness. A joyful advancement, huh? Just the loneliness of being left behind, is it? Loved me before I was born... of course, I knew that well. She was never a perfect human. She had habits and traits that sometimes, especially in my less-understanding teenage years, drove me up the wall. I guess when you are a child and you learn your parent is imperfect, for some reason it feels like much more of a letdown than finding out about anyone else's flaws. For so many years, you think they can do no wrong, that they know everything, that they always make the right decision. Maybe since those same years were spent teaching you everything that you were doing wrong and how to fix it, it felt extra satisfying to really hold over their heads just how imperfect they were.

Despite those minor imperfections that seemed so huge at the time, I never questioned her love for me. She had always listened to me with her absolute attention. If she was reading a book, she closed it the moment I started talking to her. She laughed at my silliness and my jokes, she was aware of every material need I had, and she somehow found ways to support me in all of my endeavors. And never a complaint or a sigh or a "you better be grateful." She didn't say a word about it when she was in the hospital for two weeks the year after the divorce, following a complication with a surgery, and I came to see her a grand total of one time. She never scolded me for hiding out in my room when the six and a half foot, twenty-five-year-old son of a neighbor, who had suffered brain damage during birth, was at our house so his father could go to work. She never chided me for my lack of patience with him, or my refusal to help when he wet his pants or dumped a gallon of milk on the kitchen floor. She never expressed disappointment in me when yet another neighbor with mental disabilities, a thirty-year-old woman who behaved like she was four, sent me running once again to the comfort of my bedroom. I could always hear her, clear across the house.

"Lisa! LISA! Tell Haley to make you spaghetti for dinner tonight!"

"Lisa! LISA! Call Paul and tell him to come back home and mow the lawn!"

"Lisa! LISA! Tell Suzy her room is too messy! She needs to clean it right now!"

No, instead she just became that woman's best friend. She went to get ice cream with her. She went to the play she was in with other special needs adults. She carefully wrote down notes, as dictated by her friend, and delivered them to each of us.

"Dear Haley, I love you. You are my friend."

Even when I yelled at her that she had to do something, preferably something permanent, about that dang dog! she didn't raise an eyebrow or argue back. I reached the end of my rope with Jake after he found a doll I had bought from a little old woman in a village in the Andes—handmade, down to spinning and dying the wool herself—and had torn it to shreds. After offering to drive him to the pound myself, she simply said, "If we don't love him, who will?"

And now this list. I wanted to be upset. I wanted to hurt, to be angry, to suffer and sorrow and ache. I didn't want to feel good or "get over it." I didn't want to accept things as they were now. No, I wanted them back the way they were before. Way before! I wanted to be a happy, ignorant child again, only worrying about when I'd have my next popsicle or how long I could get away with playing outside before having to come in and do chores. And she wanted me to be happy that she was gone, or at least not sad. In the end, despite myself, her words tamed my raging heart. They helped me, slowly, to move on.

We all moved on. The house finally sold, as did her car. We finally got the autopsy report back. I picked it up from the coroner, and sat in the car in the parking lot to read it. Cardiac arrest, for reasons unclear but possibly related to medications. And that was that.

Paul and Amelia had another baby. A girl, this time. Josie. Even Suzy, who had sworn herself to the life of a lone wolf as she gallivanted across the globe after graduation, met Owen a couple years later and decided that getting married was a good new adventure to start. He trained police dogs for the SWAT team, how could she resist?

And the gallivanting didn't stop—they extended their honeymoon in Ghana indefinitely, working with a humanitarian group to bring cleaner water to communities, teach English to orphans, and even to help grow crops and tend cattle.

I moved on, too. I started working at a local greenhouse. I spent my days unloading boxes and boxes of hyacinths, tulips, cacti, ornamental grasses, and so on. I did the watering and the potting as well. In the winter months especially, being around so many living things seemed to breathe the life back into me. All day long I would take slow, deep breaths, smelling the rich soil and the sweet fragrances of the plants and flowers around me. Mom used to bring me to the nursery. We would be there for what felt like hours while she carefully chose which little lives to bring home with us. That smell would linger on us for a little while after. It was therapy like nothing else so far had been able to offer. I felt the pieces of my life and my soul begin, slowly, to fuse back together.

After a few months I met Jack. We went to church together, and he seemed nice enough, but I didn't want anything to do with him. Not that there was anything wrong with him, I just didn't really want anything to do with anyone. He persisted, however, and we started spending time together, first with other friends, then alone. For our first real date, he took me out to a nearby nature conservancy where we walked and talked, enjoying the birds, the wildflowers, and popsicles.

Despite my best efforts to repel him, he found ways to break through my wall and make me feel things again. Maybe it was because at the time, I didn't care what he thought (I didn't care what anyone thought), so I could say whatever I felt like saying. Dating had always been difficult for me. Opening up, being myself—please, send me to Guantanamo instead. Jack made it easy somehow. Since losing Mom, I'd more or less become numb to everything. But he made me laugh, and he reignited my imagination. After that first walk, we went on lots of adventures that, in the magical universe we had begun to weave, were grand and exciting. It wasn't as childish as it sounds, it truly was magic. He made the cold, empty world fill up with color again.

I didn't make it easy on him. My mind was not in a place for romance, and I fought that aspect of our relationship. Even when I found out that we had the same favorite restaurant that we both *always* went to on our birthday, or when he gave me a music box he had handmade at the shop where he worked, with a butterfly burned beautifully on top, I couldn't admit that what I was feeling was real. We still disagree on whether or not it was a conscious or subconscious fight. The truth of the matter was, I had never been so at ease, so free to be myself, around anyone. Ever. I tried going on dates with other people, even some of my oldest friends, but none of them made me feel as at home as Jack did. With Jack, I felt vulnerable and exposed, and yet safe. Admitting that there was any sort of romantic tie to those feelings meant more than I was ready to process.

And yet, somehow, magically, he finally taught me how to love without hesitation and we, too, got married. We chose the Fourth of July, my favorite holiday, as our date. The ceremony was small, with just our immediate family and a few of our closest friends. Later, we had a party at Dad's house for a slightly larger crowd. There were sunflowers and strings of white lights everywhere. We served watermelon, corn on the cob, peach pie, and lemonade. There were lawn games, picnic blankets, water balloons, big band music, and, of course, fireworks. It was a perfectly joyful beginning to a new chapter.

Even Jake got to start again—my dad and stepmom graciously took him in and, after he adjusted to their tiny black kitten, of which he was terrified, he became the best he'd ever been. He got the amount of love he deserved, the kind of love my mom had given him, with the active, social lifestyle he needed. His neuroses continued, but he was in a safe, happy place with people who loved him despite it all. My dad and Lila had a way of making all of us feel loved and safe. It was another one of those blessings we couldn't have foreseen; how painful the divorce had been, but how wonderful it was to have such an incredible woman as our stepmother to fill the hole in our lives left by the death of our mother. She would never pretend to be a replacement, but she never backed down from a single role or responsibility that a biological mother would take on. I spent many months after the funeral and before I got married living with them, and just like they did for Jake, they helped me heal.

A year had passed, two, then three. It was easier now. The last time I had really cried had been Christmas Eve that first December. I was heading home after passing a lovely evening with Jack and his family, and decided to stop by the cemetery to wish Mom a Merry Christmas. I was feeling warm all over, excited and happy to be with my soulmate for the holidays. My boots crunched through the snow. It was so cold that the first inch or so was solid ice, and my foot hesitated for a moment with every step before breaking through to the sandy, powdery stuff beneath. My cheeks stung and my lungs ached with the cold air—it was what we like to call "stupid cold."

Then I reached her spot. I stood there, for a moment, staring at the marker with her name written on it. The warmth I had felt whooshed out of me and I was as cold inside as I was outside. I was suddenly overtaken by not a wave, but a tsunami of emotion. I collapsed in the snow and, between sobs, told the headstone that this wasn't fair! She should be here! It's Christmas, and she should be here, and she wasn't, and I wasn't okay with that. I wasn't okay with that! I wanted her back, right now. My grief felt uncontainable, like a reservoir whose dam had just broken. That raging sorrow, that horrible, ravaging, wretched pain filled me all over again.

After a few minutes, my body stopped shaking, and the crisp winter air cleared my head. I drew in a long, deep breath and let it out slowly, watching it form a cloud in front of my face. I stared at the clear sky, filled with dazzling stars. Then, still sniffling and with the cold biting at my face where the tears still persisted, I managed to sing one verse of Silent Night for her. My voice quivered and shook, and I wept through the whole thing. It wasn't pretty, but I felt compelled. The moon was bright overhead, and annoyingly cheerful, like it, too, was there to wish her a Merry Christmas. Resigning myself to reality, I stood, brushed the snow off my knees, blew a kiss to her memory, and stalked back to my car.

The only time after that that I had cried had been the first anniversary, the same day a nephew on Jack's side had been born. The sadness of missing my mom, coupled with the joy of a new life beginning confused me and, of course, led me to tears and silence. I don't think I looked a single soul in the eye that day. In fact, I don't think I looked anyone in the eye again until the day after when I held that new baby. He looked me right in the eye as I fed him his bottle, and things were okay again. Since then, almost nothing. Her absence was always felt, but life just...moved on. I didn't give it permission to do so, it just did, and eventually thinking of her was a comfort, not a stab of pain. Eventually, I could start to grow again.

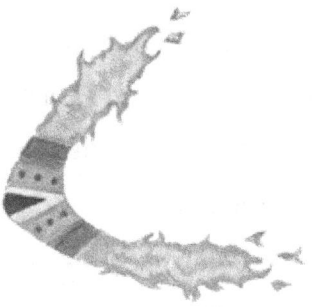

Four

Henry dodged as Eden came flying through the air past him. She hit the ground with a silent *poof* and rolled several times before leaping to her feet, straightening her ball cap, and charging back the way she had just come, bellowing a fierce war cry and baring her teeth.

The battle had been raging on for more time now than any of the soldiers had expected, following Haley wherever she went—at home, at work, in the car, while she slept. Some of the guardians had thought the worst of it had already passed. They had seen their charge through her darkest time yet, and come out overwhelmingly victorious. However, the war for Haley's soul only intensified. Made more bitter by defeat, the Opposition vengefully returned with an even greater, more vicious force. Audible only to the ears of the angels and the demons was horrible screeching, howling and hissing, punctuated by the calls and cries of the battalion. The Darkness and the Light were wrestling for dominance, and the fight was ugly and brutal.

Strong though his soldiers were, Henry's success always depended on the soul he guarded. The battalion simply could not win without her. When that light in her core dimmed and sometimes even seemed to go out, the Opposition would gain the opening they were waiting for. They would besiege her consciousness with villainous discouragement, despair, anger, and shame. Times like those—times like now—had every soldier giving their utmost. Even when the enemy won a battle the battalion never relented, never backed down, never left Haley's side for an instant. Eventually, they could always get her light going again. She, too, was relentless even in defeat. She always had been, even before mortality.

Eden and David fought side by side. The young girl and the old man made a formidable team. Her hand flew from pouch to slingshot faster than any mortal could manage, and faster than any guardian, for that matter. David's cane rained destruction on the snapping, snarling shadow beasts. He lifted it into the air and with both hands spun it around like the blades of a helicopter. A brilliant stream of light exploded from the end and flew in every direction for several yards, clearing their space and giving the two a moment to breathe. The moment they relaxed, however, the Opposition seized the opportunity to attack. The dark fog, like a tornado, screamed toward them at an alarming speed. Before they could even raise their weapons, they were swallowed up in the raging storm of hateful darkness, tumbling around within the black twister. The howling wind of evil spirits pressed upon them from every direction with all their might, churning and convulsing as it attempted to extinguish the light within the two guardians. Soon it formed a jet black sphere around them, and the final escaping beams were smothered. Eden and David's light could no longer be seen.

Nearby, Grace had seen their plight. This particular fight being more ruthless than most, she had opted for her own unique blend of ballet and wushu, a classic fighting style she had been learning from a guardian in another battalion. She headed towards Dima, dancing with beautiful form and striking with frightening power. She snapped her ribbon out to dispose of a particularly hideous six-legged, hyena-like demon sneaking up on him, then, after getting his attention, directed it towards the faintly glowing orb, floating a few inches off the ground. With a swipe of his rapier, he finished the ugly snake-faced demon he had been fighting. He gave his weapon a quick, hard shake and it became an aboriginal boomerang. He took a couple quick breaths and focused intently on the orb, while Grace danced around him protectively. He had seen this happen once before, when he first became a guardian. The captain he had had then told him it was a dangerous, desperate move—one that told you at the same time that you were winning, and that you were in deep trouble. While it left the enemy vulnerable, such an attempt to smother a guardian was a wild and violent move, and meant that the enemy wasn't holding back any of its rage or thirst for destruction. Dima closed his eyes and whispered something to the boomerang, which, in response, burst into heavenly flames. The fire was silent and soft, but had a fierceness and a determination in its angelic light. After positioning himself in a steady stance, Dima hurled it expertly towards the black ball trapping his fellow guardians. Leaving a resplendent trail like a comet, the boomerang flew through the air, slicing through its target. For a moment, nothing happened. Then, it came flying back out to him just in time for him to catch it, snap it in half and give the pieces another shake. He used the resulting pair of sai to do battle with new demons that had arrived. The dark spirits flooded in around him, sensing his strength, eager to destroy it.

"Cute, baby pitchforks!" Grace commented innocently as she lunged low to duck the swinging arm of a demon that reminded her of the gorillas she had seen at the zoo with her mom. Dima rolled his eyes.

For a moment, the black orb seemed to have been unaffected by the boomerang's strike. Then, like rays of sunshine splitting a stormy sky, the Darkness began to fracture and tear. The glowing cracks were quickly swallowed up again with voracious, swirling black fog, but just as soon as they were filled, more and more appeared until finally, after a shuddering, furious attempt to stay whole, it exploded into a hailstorm of brilliant, starlike light. With a howl, the enemy withdrew to regroup. Eden, who had been forced to her knees, stood, brushing herself off. A thick coat of ebony dust covered her and her elderly partner. She pulled David to his feet and with a grin brushed off his shoulders and coaxed a triumphant high-five out of the old soldier. David shook his head and chuckled. Eden grabbed his cane from off the ground and handed it to him.

"Let's get 'em," she said with a wicked grin and a flame behind her glaring eyes. David straightened his bowtie.

"Indeed, let's."

As usual, Henry was at his post at Haley's side. They were

in her bedroom, though the walls and furniture were little more than faint shadows to the battalion. She was standing in front of a full-length mirror, and while there were no tears in her eyes this time, her teeth were clenched and her eyes were empty but for a hint of disgust. Henry looked in the mirror, and the reflection he saw was brilliant. Her whole body seemed to glow, her eyes were sharp, alert, and bright. Her head was held high, her shoulders were strong, and her mouth was curved in a small smile that was confident and joyful. He looked back to Haley, and saw her the way she saw herself. There was no glow. Everything, even her skin and her eyes, seemed grey and dull. There was nothing exciting or alive about her, certainly nothing confident. Henry looked back to the reflection, which showed her the way he always remembered her. His teeth were clenched now, too.

"See what you are!" he yelled over the raucous din. He could faintly hear Stephanie's warm, sweet voice singing one of Haley's favorite lullabies. The Darkness surrounded the captain and his charge. It could not touch Haley, but it pulled at Henry, trying to drag him away from her. He swung his golden sword this way and that, refusing to be moved. Ugly, deformed faces appeared in the heavy, black fog, jeering at Henry and whispering in Haley's ear.

"Worthless. Plain. Helpless. Useless. Failure. Undone."

"NO!" shouted Henry, jerking his arm out of the grasp of another fiendish creature. "Battalion! RALLY!"

Almost instantly, Eden, David, Dima, and two other soldiers, a middle-aged man with glasses and a cheerful face, and a woman even older than David with perfectly permed hair, appeared at his side. Henry always had his core of soldiers that were assigned to his battalion, but in particularly difficult times, extra help often appeared. A moment later, they were joined by Grace, Stephanie, and a young boy, about twelve years old with wildly curly blond hair and a sweet face with just a hint of mischief in his bright eyes.

David and Grace fought off the enemy while Henry spoke with the battalion. Wary of the entire group of guardians gathered so tightly, the demons hesitated briefly. Only a few darted forward to attack, and they were met and destroyed by the fierce guards. The enemy retreated for a moment, quickly gathering a force that could take on the concentrated strength of the battalion.

"Henry, this isn't working," Eden said calmly as she loaded a glowing marble into the pouch on her slingshot. She aimed and let it fly at a charging demon with huge tusks.

"Stay close. Look out for each other. Jack is coming. He's got to be coming, we just have to hold out until then. This is a fight Haley has to join, she can't hide, she can't sit on the sidelines like she does sometimes. This is one *she* has to win. We can only do so much. Don't be discouraged," he added, as he saw Eden's shoulders fall a little, "we're on the winning side. We're always on the winning side. We just have to keep them from overwhelming her, let her think clearly and keep control of her feelings. Now, go!"

The battalion dispersed, and not a moment too soon. The demons that had hesitated with some trepidation for those few seconds had overcome their fear as they had been joined by more devilish beings. They readied themselves and charged yet again. David and Grace were about to be engulfed in the swarming horde, but just in time the old lady and the young boy joined them, the first armed with two flaming knitting needles and the second with a glowing baseball bat. Together, the four of them held their position strong.

"We need more help!" Dima shouted from across the room as the Opposition snaked its way between him and Eden. Darkness began again to overwhelm the valiant warriors, despite their incredible effort. A swarm of small, winged demons dove in formation at one guardian after another. Their screeches were high-pitched and piercing. Weapons were swinging so rapidly that they blurred as they flew through one opponent after another. The Opposition multiplied faster than they could destroy it. Henry wished he could call on the Light beings again and use their combined energy to annihilate the entire force raging against them, like they had done once before, but he knew he couldn't. He had to let Haley fight. He would fight, too, with all his might, but he couldn't always take it out of her hands. He had to let her try, even if it meant sometimes letting her fail. It was her battle, after all, not his.

"Embarrassment. You don't deserve him. You aren't even pretty. You have no talent. You are worthless."

"No, Haley, no! Look at yourself! *See* who you are!" Henry commanded. He took her by the shoulders, searching her eyes for some sign of light, some small glimmer of hope. He wanted to shake her, to grab her face and force her to see him, and then to see the stunning reflection behind him. But, of course, he couldn't. She didn't feel his hands on her shoulders. She didn't hear his cries.

One of the many faces that had been materializing from the fog clung to its shape longer than the rest. It stretched and writhed as it pulled itself free of the vile cloud. As the rest of a body began to form below it, the other demons shrieked with fear and shrank back, like lesser predators relenting a kill to the more dominant hunter. In a moment, the figure of a slender, wicked looking man stood next to Henry. His form shifted and wavered, but held. Though flickering like the flame of a candle, his spirit body was as clear and detailed as Henry's. Frightening in his clarity, he looked pityingly from Henry to Haley.

"Tisk, tisk," he sighed with mock disappointment. His smooth, soft voice sounded like a distant hiss. It was unnerving and thick with enmity. "You aren't worried, are you, Captain?"

Henry's spirit was suddenly filled with echoes of feelings he had once had, feelings of coldness and dread, of despair and desolation. He knew this demon well. With a furious yell, he swung his sword. The figure vanished just in time, only to reappear on his other side. He was dressed in a fine, black suit. His face was of an older, handsome man, with a crooked grin and narrowed eyes. His voice was simpering and slippery, and all too familiar.

"Worried a 'Great One' might just tumble and fall?" He said the title with unmistakable derision, and for a moment his crooked grin turned to a nasty scowl. "It's happened many times before, you know. It will happen again."

"Leave her be," Henry seethed. The demon's grin returned, all the more wicked, and it leaned in towards Haley.

"She'll give up eventually, Henry. She'll realize how worthless she is, how pointless it all is, this 'trying to be better' nonsense. She'll finally accept the fact that she's just a *stupid girl*," he hissed.

"Stupid," Haley muttered under her breath. She glared into her own reflection's eyes and Henry could see her disgust with what she saw become uglier and meaner. The demon stretched out his hand, finger nails long and sharp, to touch Haley's face. But before he could reach her, Henry roared and plunged his sword into the monstrous devil's core. The demon let out a shriek which turned into maniacal laughter, and like the last of the bathwater, he swirled around and around Henry's sword before vanishing. He was gone, but Henry knew it was only temporary.

Suddenly, through the Darkness, a light appeared in the distance, moving towards them. Henry's heart leaped. Finally. Reinforcements.

"He's coming! They're coming! Hold on, everyone!"

The bedroom door opened, and Jack, weary but cheerful, entered.

"What a day! You wouldn't believe what the chief..." He paused upon seeing Haley, instantly aware of what was going on. He crossed over to her and wrapped his arms around her. She tried to shrug him off, unwilling to be comforted, but he held tight. She persisted.

"Don't touch me, Jack. I just...need some space."

He didn't understand why she felt the way she did about herself, since he saw nothing but beauty, talent, strength, and worth. He knew it wasn't his job to understand, so much as it was to do everything he could to counter those feelings with words and acts to disprove them. Even so, he still felt helpless most of the time. He was still learning what things worked and what things just made it worse.

"I don't know what demons you're fighting, Love, but I'm not going anywhere. Whatever it takes to work through this and beat it, I'll do it."

Jack was accompanied by his own battalion, strong and ready. They came in, weapons already raised, and immediately joined the fight. His captain battled through the melee to Henry. As she neared, the light that glowed in his chest immediately grew.

"Beth," he sighed with relief. She smiled warmly, and her bright, beautiful face filled Henry with courage and determination greater than he already had. She was petite, but strong, and strapped around her waist was a belt with a sheath on either side, each holding a small, deadly sword. Her deep blue eyes shone with emotion as they took in Henry.

"I'm sorry it took us so long to get here. He was busy. Work is taking its toll," she explained. Her chestnut hair hung in a long braid over her shoulder, which she tossed behind her back as she unsheathed both of her weapons. A tall, strapping young man, with eyes just like Beth's, appeared at her side. For a moment, Henry was grateful not to have a body, otherwise he was sure his knees would have given out and his heart would have exploded with the joy he felt in their presence. Again, the echoes of such strong feelings made his spirit body tremble.

"Benjamin," Henry breathed with a smile. He saw them almost every day, but the feelings he had at the sight of their faces never dulled.

"We're here, Dad," said Benjamin, smiling though clearly having just come from a battle of his own. "What can we do?"

"Just get Jack talking. She needs to hear him. I'm not getting through."

"Right away," said Beth, and with a wink and a smile, she turned to leave. At the last second, she turned back around. "Oh, and Henry?"

"Yes?"

"We brought a secret weapon." She winked again and hurried back to Jack, who was patiently listening to Haley.

"I'm so lost, Jack!" she was yelling. "Sometimes I hate who I am, but I don't know why. I know I'm a good person, so why do I feel like this? What is so terrible about me that makes me feel this way? I hate that I don't know! I hate that I can't control it! I hate this, Jack!" she yelled. Her raging turned against herself quickly and with biting disgust.

Before Henry could call Beth back to ask about the secret weapon, another bright form came out of the darkness towards him. The kindly woman who had visited him at his mountain home stood before him, still smiling that sweet smile.

"You're back," he said, glad to see her, but anxious to get back to the fight. He didn't see any sort of weapon in her hands, so he was sure she wasn't there to stay.

"Just for a moment. I brought some friends along that I thought might help you. Secret weapons, as Beth likes to call them." She stepped to the side so Henry could see behind her. There, sitting in a single file line behind her, was a whole pack of dogs, varying in breed and size but all glowing warmly. They wagged their tails whenever a guardian came near, and bore their teeth at the demons, who instantly began avoiding them. David, who was nearest, ended his current match with a powerful swing of his cane, then turned to bow reverently towards the dogs, all of whom had to restrain themselves with great difficulty from rushing over to him.

"That's Jesse, Max, Asia, Abby, Lotty, Jag, and Gunner," said the woman. "I got special permission to bring them along."

Henry stared, incredulous. "How did you—"

"Nevermind that," she said with a pleased smile. "Now, they all have other assignments, but this one—" she pointed to a giant black lab, "—has been reassigned to your battalion indefinitely. His name is Jag. Haley's going to need her strength. This is certainly not the last or the worst fight we'll have like this." She turned to the dogs. "No one else could do for her quite what you did. Now do it again!"

Immediately, like someone had thrown a ball or a frisbee, they were off, each in a different direction.

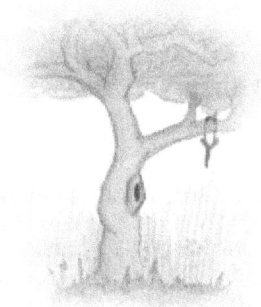

Five

The sun was hot on my neck as I stormed up the mountain, disregarding my burning lungs and aching legs. I welcomed the discomfort, felt worthy of the pain. The steeper the trail was, the better. I slipped and twisted my ankle—good. A branch scratched my arm—fine. I marched up, up, up.

It had been another difficult morning. I didn't know why this kept happening. It had been three years since Mom died, and almost two since Jack and I were married. My brain had moved on, my life had moved on, but my emotions seemed locked in that horrible summer when it all happened. For some reason, I was stuck. I had been broken, and I couldn't seem to recover and be my normal, happy self again. There were lots of happy moments, even entire days and weeks. I kept thinking that I was okay—finally, okay—but then something would set me off. Something small, like losing the keys or a bad hair day.

I remember vividly the moment I decided that I wanted to be a happy person. I was probably about six years old. I must have been acting like a real terror, because my siblings tattled on me and Mom pulled me into her room, just the two of us.

"I don't know who this girl is," she said. I had expected to be in big trouble, but she didn't seem angry. Just...sad. "Where's my happy Haley?"

My six-year-old self had found it easy to dispel bad feelings. I was still emotional, sensitive, sometimes even a little wicked, but I was resolved to be Mom's Happy Haley. My twenty-five-year-old self wasn't having such an easy time of it.

That particular morning I had ended up on the mountain because I was raging again, and Jack had handed me my backpack and my shoes and pushed me out the door.

"Go to the mountain and don't come back until you can be nice to yourself," he had ordered. When I raged, it was almost always at myself. Nothing about me was good enough, and I couldn't forgive myself for it. I am a nice person, but if anyone had heard or seen the way I behaved towards myself on those bad days, they would have been horrified.

So, I was banished to the mountain. Jack knew it was a place where I forgot to hate me, and so there I was sent. I was still mad when I arrived, though. You can't just demand happiness from me. I was mad, and I wanted to explode and I wanted to hit things and I wanted to break things. I can't just not feel what I feel, I can't just turn it off and be happy.

Instead of enjoying the mountain, I was bent on conquering it, and half hoped it would conquer me, too, just to prove to Jack that I really was useless. I hadn't taken more than a few steps before my face was wet with tears. After a while, as I stormed up and up the trail, the tears dried and I was left with empty, hollow anger again. Up, up, up the mountain. Up, up, up.

Step after step, my lungs protested and my legs begged for a break, but I refused to give them any respite. My anger grew more wild, my loathing for myself more vicious. I couldn't give any good reason for my emotions, I knew I was a good person. I cared about people, I served others, I visited my grandparents, I baked cookies for friends I knew were struggling. I knew I had wonderful things to offer the world—I was smart and driven and creative. Yet, still there was this wretched, bitter loathing rooted in me that seemed to have no source. The fact that there was no logic to my feelings only fanned the furious flames.

Finally, when my lungs were certain to burst, I stopped next to a large pine tree. Heaving for air, and feeling like the entire world must hate me as much as I did, I let out a cry of rage and pounded the tree with my fist three times as hard as I could. My legs gave out and I fell to the ground, leaning against the poor victim of my outburst. The tears were back, and though desperate, seemed more cleansing than anything. After a few minutes, my body started to relax and the streams flowing from my eyes started to slow. My hands, still tightly clenched in fists and throbbing painfully, relaxed.

Rogue strands of hair danced on my face in the cool, light breeze. I could hear the soothing trickling and babbling of the creek nearby. Here, in the shade, the sun seemed less like it was trying to fry me alive and more like a thoughtful friend attempting to cheer me up. I didn't want to be cheered up. A squirrel ran down the tree on the other side, I could almost hear him humming as he skipped along. Upon coming around the trunk to find me sitting there, he froze, slowly backed up a few steps, then darted away as fast as he could. My scowl cracked slightly, and I wanted to laugh as I heard, in my imagination, his hysterical, squirrely scream. Then I remembered I was mad, and forced the emotion back to the surface. I heard Jack's voice in my head.

"Uh, oh—are your grumpies getting frustrated?"

I let out an irritated scoff. I hated it when he said that. Just thinking about it made my temper spike like a solar flare. Any time I suddenly lost my reason for being upset, or was unexpectedly comforted or encouraged, he would say that and I would want so badly to still be angry or sad just to prove that no such thing was happening. My feelings were so deeply set and so volatile. It felt to me like if I could change them on a dime, they couldn't be real, or reasonable, or rational, and so I shouldn't have them in the first place. If they weren't real, how could I fix them? How could I beat them, move past them? Burying them wouldn't help. I needed them to be real, to be validated, tangible, so that I could conquer them. Otherwise it would just mean that I was crazy. Like a fever, I had to let them run their course.

Jack was right, though. On regular occasion, my grumpies *were* frustrated, and I was cured of my mood. It wasn't that I didn't want to be happy, I was simply terrified that it meant my emotions weren't valid. They assaulted me with such ferocity and so often, they left me emotionally crippled and spiritually scarred. They had to be real. Nothing that wasn't real could have such a devastating effect.

What was it Mom had said in her list? Peace and happiness can be yours whenever you want it enough? So did that mean that since I was feeling so low and so hopeless so often that I just didn't want to be happy? What did I have to do to want it more than I already did? All I knew was I did *not* want to feel the way I was right then. I *did* want my grumpies frustrated! But I also didn't want to feel crazy, or like I was choosing to be miserable and upset. When I was happy, I wanted to do whatever it took to keep it that way. I loved my life, I really did. But why? Why did I love my life if I felt like I was drowning in it just as often, if not more, than not?

That day, on the mountain, perspective, gradually at first and then more quickly, came flooding back to me. I thought of a friend of mine whose three-year-old daughter was in the hospital for her third open-heart surgery. I thought of a recent earthquake in South America and the devastating toll it had taken on the people there. I thought of the home I had—with clean running water, air conditioning and heat, soft carpet, a washer and dryer and all other modern conveniences, not to mention the full refrigerator and pantry, toilet paper, ice cubes, and two whole bedrooms, just for me and Jack. I was exquisitely blessed, and those were just some of my physical blessings. My mind was almost overwhelmed as I thought of all the things I had to be grateful for—a car, a bank account, shoes to wear, a shower every day, electricity, family, friends, health, God…

I felt my mind coming back to me. I think what my mom meant was that as long as I didn't give up, as long as I refused to give in to whatever was attacking me, peace and happiness would always, *always*, be back. They would never be lost unless I let them go. The dark cloud that seemed to engulf me dissipated. Those thoughts I would have, those mean and nasty thoughts, weren't my own. They weren't coming from me. I spent enough time in church growing up and through my brief adult years up to that point to know that opposition is necessary. Because we know what sadness is, we can know joy. Because we know pain, we can know pleasure. Because I could feel the derision and scorn of Satan, I could also feel and know the love of God. He loved me, I knew that, and He was aware of every detail of my life. His plan for me was one of happiness, but it would require some work, some struggle, some growth.

I filled my lungs with the clean, fresh mountain air and felt like it was the first breath I had taken all day. I tossed a handful of sunflower seeds from my backpack to the little squirrel that poked his head out from around the tree again, and headed down the mountain. If I was experiencing such awful, cruel opposition, it must mean that something wonderful was coming. I didn't want my life to be an angry, frustrated, discouraged one. Every time the light came back on in my soul, after I was sure it was out for good, I knew I could try again. I knew I wasn't done for yet.

On the day of the funeral, two swallowtail butterflies had been floating around, silently, calmly. They landed on the casket and stayed there for a long time. They seemed to step so carefully, to move so reverently. All three of us siblings noticed them. Ever since, the swallowtail has represented our mom. Sometimes, when I was having particularly difficult days, or even on good days, one would suddenly be there. It would flutter past my face or land nearby and I would remember her with a feeling of peace. She wasn't here anymore, that was true and I would eventually come to accept it. But, she wasn't exactly gone either.

On my way down the mountain that morning, there seemed to be a veritable army of swallowtail butterflies, one appearing just as the other disappeared. Escorted all the way to my car by the winged beauties, I headed home to start the day over again. Something good was coming. It had to be.

September 3, 1992

Dearest Haley,

I can't quite believe that you are so big already. Time goes by so quickly. These little childhood years seem to be slipping through my fingers much more rapidly than I'd like. I enjoy you so very much. One of my favorite things is to take you with me somewhere alone. You are great company and you keep me laughing constantly with your very deep three-year-old thoughts—"Mom, do our arms bug us?" and your witty quips—"Saying shut up is a big rudeness, huh Mom." "I think I'm going to be four in fifteen minutes."

I am truly grateful every day to be your mother. I could not be happier or feel more blessed.

You are a very spunky little thing. You are very opinionated and strong willed, but fortunately, you usually eventually submit to reason. But not always. You like to do absolutely everything that Paul does, and insist that you can do it better and faster. You are an amazing combination of feisty and shy, of vulnerability and invincibility. You easily win people over, but those hands go on your hips and that little foot stomps if someone steps over the line. You are the oldest in your preschool group, but the smallest. Sometimes I trick myself into thinking that you are fragile, because you tire easily, and you are always cold. But you are tough. *Anyone who thinks you're a shy little floofy-fluff (and many people do, because you are so petite and have those great, big Bambi-brown eyes) has got another thing coming.*

One of your favorite things to do right now is to feed the dogs. I don't know if it is really that fascinating, or if it is just a ploy to get yourself outside. You just love to be outside—no matter the weather or time of day. Last week you talked and pleaded until you finally got me to come out and sit on the bench on the front porch and eat a popsicle with you while the rain poured down around us.

You always say exactly what you think. If anyone offends you, you go nose to nose with them and tell them exactly what is wrong with them—kind of like a Marine Corps drill sergeant. And heaven forbid that anyone should really offend you, because you hold a grudge forever.

You are very imaginative. I suppose all little children are to some extent, but you play in a fantasy land all of the time. Your utensils become people, as do cut up pieces of paper, or food on your plate, and you have a "friend ghost" which is sometimes with you. One time last winter Daddy and I took you, Paul, and Suzy for a drive to get out of the fog. Well, eventually we turned the music tape off and just listened to you pretend in the backseat for two hours without coming back to reality until we drove back in the driveway. You like to sing a lot of your dialogues. In fact, one of the funniest things that you have done lately happened a few weeks ago. You were being cross and feisty with Paul, and you had been warned twice to talk nicely. Finally I brought you in the kitchen and sat you on a chair in the middle of the floor to think about solving problems in a nice way. Pretty soon I hear this sad little sing song voice coming from the kitchen. You were lying upside down with your legs draped over the back of the chair, tears streaming down your face, singing your tale of woes. I tip-toed back out, then about split a gut laughing, but at the same time I wanted to scoop you up and kiss your little face.

It has been a fun summer. Dad built you kids a cute little playhouse in the backyard, which you all painted "plum purple." We are raising baby chicks right now, which you have really enjoyed. We have five fluffy things in the run right now, and twenty-eight eggs incubating on my kitchen counter. We have to turn these darn eggs three times a day.

The other day, you came back from our next door neighbors' and you were telling me about what you did. "We rode around in the back of Chris' truck and fed the horses. We fed a brown one, and a white one, and a blue one, and a black one." "Oh, Haley, I didn't know that there was such a thing as a blue horse." "I know Mom, that's because you've never seen one." End of conversation—onto something else.

Well, I've been up in the night writing this. But it's starting to get light outside, and the rooster (Drumstick—we hate him) is crowing. It's time to wake everyone. Until next time,

I love you infinity,

Mom

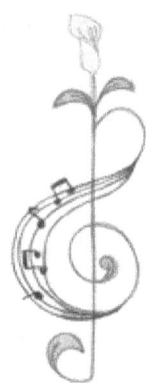

Six

Swish...pop! Swish...pop! Swish...pop!

Grace's golden ribbon was stretched out long and wide to form a net, while one of Eden's shining marbles hopped over it, back and forth, as Dima and Stephanie swatted at it with rackets made of air and imagination. Deadly in battle, the marble now was light as air and twinkling happily. With every swing, Dima's racket changed form. First a round badminton racket, then a tennis racket, then a golf club, then a baseball bat. Stephanie caught each volley with her own racket gracefully and with little effort, sending it flying back over the net for Dima to chase.

David, meanwhile, stood next to Haley. She was at work in the greenhouse, watering the pansies. They were all in full bloom, and the wealth of color was stunning. David had been quite the gardener himself in his day, so he happily took watch duty while the others, although staying nearby, enjoyed a moment of relaxation. Something about their most recent battle had seemed to discourage the enemy, or at least force them to regroup, and the respite for the Battalion was welcomed. They knew it was temporary and probably brief, but that didn't bother them. If the battle never ended, they would have kept fighting without a thought and certainly without complaint.

"Look out, you missed that one in the corner," David said to Haley. His voice couldn't reach her ears, yet her arm swung back with the hose and sprayed the forgotten corner. "There we go. Can't leave anyone out now, can we?"

The opaque dome-like building caught the sunlight and bred warmth. Though the air outside had begun to mellow from winter's biting frost to spring's milder spirit, it still had a bit of a chill in it. Inside the greenhouse, Haley eagerly and thankfully shed her jacket and hat and basked in the sweet, humid heat. She felt her body start to thaw, the blood start to flow again. There were several different buildings to the greenhouse, and though all of them were modest in size, each of them was a beloved sanctuary. There were plants hanging in pots from the ceiling, tall grasses reaching for the roof, small blooms peeking out from under rich dirt, and pallets upon pallets of glorious flowers just waiting to spread their roots and shine. Haley's shift started an hour before they opened, so she was able to enjoy the quiet company of the plants all by herself. It was her favorite hour of the day.

Grace had been practicing her Wushu training. The guardian that was teaching her was an enchanting older Chinese woman who almost never spoke, but gently corrected and demonstrated technique to Grace with great patience and skill. Without the limitations of a physical body, Grace was learning quickly and her own skill was growing exponentially. It felt like dancing, though much fiercer. Now, however, she was taking a break and lying on her belly on top of one of the pallets of dazzling hyacinths. She tried with all her might to smell one.

"Almost!" she said quietly with a big, deep inhale. Henry was sitting across the aisle next to the sunflowers, which towered over him and reached towards Grace. He smiled warmly.

"You get used to it," he told her. "After a while, once you get a little more used to your spirit body, you'll start to remember things— smells, textures, even tastes. We call them echoes."

Grace was the newest member of his battalion, and the fighting had been so constant and so intense that he had hardly had a chance to get to know her since she joined them. Most of the guardians had been through one or two battalions before this one, but she was brand new. Her legs were sticking up in the air and swaying. She rested her chin on her arms and sighed.

"Echoes…" she repeated. She sighed again.

Henry nodded with another warm smile, his gaze drifting back to Haley and David. The old man was watching the hose to make sure it didn't knock over any of the pansies as she pulled it back to the wall to hang it up on a hook. Henry stiffened as he saw a pair of demons appear. Like smoke, they slid silently into the greenhouse and underneath the tables holding the plants, trying to sneak up on Haley and her protector. Without even looking, David pointed his cane at the beasts like a gun, and a beam of light shot out of the bottom, causing one of them to explode instantly and the other to squeal and howl as it retreated with haste. Henry relaxed. He wasn't sure why there was a lull in the war for Haley's soul right now, but he was grateful for it. Though his troops were free from their imperfect, mortal bodies, they were still human, and a rest was much needed.

Jag, the big dog that had joined them during the last battle, ambled over from where he had been sitting, watching the golden ball fly back and forth with great interest, and laid down next to Grace. She threw her arms around him and buried her face in his fur. He grinned, his tongue fell limply to one side of his mouth, and his eyes narrowed as he enjoyed the snuggle. Grace pulled away from him and gave another sigh.

"Almost," she said, willing an echo of the feeling of soft fur to come to her.

"Just be patient. Someday, we will be able to see, smell, and touch everything all over again, only better than we did before."

"What about taste?" Grace asked with concern.

"Yes, I forgot, taste, too."

Grace sighed, this time with relief.

"Good. I miss chocolate. So did you know Haley even when she was a baby?" she asked Henry. He nodded.

"And long before that. But yes, I was there the day she was born," he replied.

"She must have been a beautiful baby!" Grace exclaimed. Henry's smile crinkled his eyes as he remembered.

"She was indeed. She fussed quite a lot at first—leaving heaven is harder for some than for others."

"Was she a good girl, when she was little?"

"Oh, yes. Though, she was awfully curious and always busy, which lead to a lot of mischief. She would get quite frustrated with her small body for not cooperating with her big ideas."

Grace grinned. "We probably would have been friends."

Henry nodded, amused.

"I'm sure you would have. She doesn't get to see you, but you are her friend now. She'll recognize you, when she sees you."

"Oh, yeah, I know that!" Grace said, swinging her legs around to sit up. "When I came here, I saw Millie, and I didn't know her before, but I think I knew her forever, just forgot."

"Millie was your battalion's captain?"

"Yeah. She's *beautiful*! I think all guardians are beautiful. Especially Stephanie. How long will I be a guardian?"

"Good question, Grace. None of us really know. Some of us will be guardians for a long time, until every person that will be born, has been born. Some get reassigned. Remember Lisa?"

Grace's face scrunched up as she tried to remember, then sprung back with a bright smile as she threw her arms around the big black dog again.

"She brought Jag!"

"That's right," Henry said, grinning again. He found that his smile never seemed to have time to fade before Grace caused it to return. "Lisa has many assignments. She doesn't have a battalion she stays with all the time—she gets to help us, and Paul's battalion, and Suzy's, too. And, she's on the butterfly committee. Someday you might have a different job."

"Oh, but I like this one! Millie gave me my ribbon, it's like magic, and I get to dance whenever I want to, and I never even feel tired or sick!"

"Trust me, you won't get a job you don't like."

There was a lull in their conversation as Grace nuzzled Jag and he contentedly accepted her affection. Then, her expression became troubled.

"Henry?" she asked tentatively, as though perhaps she wasn't sure she should ask what she wanted to ask.

"Yes?" he replied, curious at her tone.

"Who was that man? The one that was talking to you and trying to get Haley? The really scary one? I saw him while we were fighting last time. Most of the time, those...things...well, they just kind of look like smoke. But he kind of looked like you and me."

Henry could tell she was frightened at the memory of the demon, and he wasn't sure how to respond in a way that wouldn't frighten her further.

"His name is Daniel, which, ironically, means 'God is my judge'."

"Like Daniel from the Bible?"

"No—well, yes, same name, but a very different person."

"So who is he?" Her curiosity was overpowering her earlier prudence, and Henry could see she wasn't going to stop asking questions until he gave her some answers. He drew in a long, slow breath.

"You know how we're all a battalion, and I get to be the

captain?" he asked. Grace nodded. "Well, it's sort of the same thing with the other side. Daniel is like the captain of the other side that is trying to make Haley unhappy."

"Oh," said Grace, understanding filling her face, only to be promptly replaced by the same quizzical expression she had worn a moment before. "If he's after Haley, why was he being so mean to you?"

Henry let out a short laugh, amazed at her skills of observation.

"Well, Grace, he was the captain of the Opposition that worked against me when I was alive," he replied, convinced that he wouldn't get away with withholding anything from her at this point.

"Oh," said Grace, understanding once again flooding her expression. After a moment, her understanding turned to a troubled, almost frightened look.

"Are you alright?" Henry asked, worried he had upset her somehow.

"Yes, it's just...well, I'm just remembering something. When I met Millie, there was someone else there, too. I forgot about him, though. He sort of wasn't really there, kind of hiding in the dark. He sure looked mean. And angry! I forgot about him, because Millie was so beautiful and she was telling me so many amazing things, but I remember now..."

Henry nodded slowly.

"Some demons can't move on. Daniel was there when I first came here, too." He paused for a moment, recalling the encounter. When he died, the first thing he was aware of was a voice. It was quiet and calm, yet Henry knew he had never heard anything more powerful. He didn't comprehend fully what it was saying, but it was an unmistakable expression of love. Next, Henry saw light, and a stunning, glowing figure in the middle of it—he knew instantly that she was the captain of his very own battalion. There was someone else there, too. Unlike Grace's demon, who had lurked in the shadows, Daniel had strode out into the blazing light of Henry's guardian, who had a bow in her hand and a fiery sword at her side. He was barely visible, and though he looked feeble and weak in the glorious, bright presence of the captain, Henry recognized the intense, awful feelings coming from him. Everything unpleasant he had felt in his life, every despairing, angry, dark moment resurfaced in the company of that being. His captain had allowed Daniel to stay for a few moments, gripping her bow tightly. Henry could see his mouth moving, his lips curled and almost snarling as he screamed horrible things Henry couldn't hear. Daniel stretched his long, sharp finger towards him, pointing at the humble soul with a hatred that was monstrous and filthy.

"Now that you know him, you don't need to be afraid of him anymore," she had told him. With one deft, sweeping move, she drew, nocked, and released a fiery arrow that banished the demon back to the black shadows. Henry recalled the brief look of frustration on her beautiful, young face, which was quickly replaced with confidence. "He may never leave you be, but he can never defeat you."

Coming out of his memory, Henry looked at Grace, who still seemed troubled.

"You know, Grace, they had a choice once, the Opposition. We all did. We could choose light, or dark. You and me, we chose light.

Those things that fight Haley, and that fought you and me when we were alive, they chose dark. Sometimes I think they must be sad—"

"Because they made a bad choice? Mom taught me about conseh...conseh…"

"Consequences, exactly. They made a bad choice, and the consequences of that choice make them angry and jealous. They missed out on the chance to live a mortal life, to experience a body, a family, everything. Even when you are done with your life on Earth, they don't want to leave you alone, because you have something they don't, and never will. You have hope. I think Daniel is very sad, and therefore very angry, and so he wants to keep hurting me now, just like he wants to hurt Haley."

Grace's expression was extremely grave as she contemplated this.

"But we won't ever stop fighting for her, will we?" said Henry encouragingly.

Grace grinned.

"Never!"

Just then, the golden marble fell out of nowhere, right in front of Grace's nose. She jumped and let out a yelp of surprise, and Dima ran over to scoop it up with a lacrosse stick.

"Sorry!" he said as he rushed back to the game.

Grace's eyes were wide and her smile was enormous. Her hands flew to her heart and she bounced up and down with glee.

"My heart! It did a loopty-loop!"

"An echo," Henry beamed, his own heart swelling.

Seven

    I remember the first time someone told me they thought I was struggling with depression. It was when I was in Mexico volunteering during my first summer after high school. She was one of the leaders of our group, sort of the matron.

    "Or maybe anxiety? I'm not sure, Haley, all I know is you're dealing with something, and you don't have to do it on your own. There are people...professionals...who can help you."

    Immediately, my mind revolted at the idea. My insides felt like they were a pile of squirming worms, I felt unsettled and upset, even offended. Still, she contacted my parents and told them her concerns.

    Mom didn't say much. I didn't realize it at the time, but I suspect now that she had been battling her own depression for several years. Dad said it was a bunch of garbage, I wasn't depressed, I just didn't like being there and should come home.

That was what most people said. "Haley? Depressed? Please." Happy Haley, right? And to be honest, I agreed with them. Sure, I had some tough times, but most of the time I was completely fine. Honestly, completely fine. When I came home, though, somehow someone convinced my parents to try some therapy and some medications. I had three or four sessions with a psychologist, who was a strange older man with a small face, pointy nose, and big glasses. He was nice, and seemed to know a lot about psychology, but nothing he said made me feel better. In fact, I felt worse. I left his office feeling defiant and annoyed. How dare he tell me what I am feeling and why? He didn't know me. He didn't understand me. He pried into every detail of my life, and I unwillingly divulged. Even then, he drew conclusions that enraged me.

The therapy was bad, but the medication was a nightmare. They told me sometimes things get worse before they get better, that I needed to give it at least six weeks. For four weeks, I took one tiny white pill every day, hating it, knowing with absolute certainty that it would not fix me, furious that everyone seemed to think I was broken in the first place. For four weeks I felt unrelenting bitterness and debilitating frustration. I know that medication is miraculous for some people, I know it can turn their entire life right side up again. It did not have that effect on me.

Finally, I told them I wouldn't do it anymore. I wouldn't take one more pill. They told me I shouldn't go off it suddenly, and they were probably right, but whatever bad side effects might have come seemed to be offset by the relief I felt at closing the bottle for the last time. The doctors suggested we try a different medication. No, I said, and my parents agreed. Never again, I promised myself.

I created my own therapy. I went hiking almost every day. I made a conscious effort to serve others. I chose healthy food and drank lots of water. I tried to get plenty of sleep. I prayed constantly. It helped. I'd go weeks and weeks feeling good, feeling normal, feeling like I had conquered whatever the problem had been. Then, out of the blue, I would trip and fall into a deep, dark pit of agonizing despair. The smallest thing would set it off. Sometimes there would be a day or two with a few mishaps or disappointments leading up to it, and then all of the sudden I would break into a million pieces. It felt like my insides had melted, like I could barely move, like my vision was distorted so that I could only see a few feet in front of me, everything else was engulfed in a mean, black fog. I couldn't think, I could barely speak. Everything I did was wrong, everything I did was bad. For no reason at all, I wanted to cry and scream and break things. For no reason at all, I felt impossibly low, impossibly worthless. Eventually it would pass, and once again I would climb out of the hole and start to believe I had beat whatever it was, perhaps this time for good.

After I married Jack, I thought those times were finally behind me. Finally, with my other half at my side, I would truly have no reason to sorrow so deeply, to ache so profoundly. The first time it happened after we were together, I panicked, thinking something was wrong with our relationship. We worked through it, and I was sure that we were stronger for it. But, any time there was any conflict between us, I immediately assumed it was my fault. I was out of control with my emotions, so it was my fault. It had to be.

If Jack didn't refute my claim to guilt instantly and definitively, then I felt angry at him for letting me beat myself up. He should be defending me, he should be protecting me, even if it meant he had to protect me from myself. When he did, though, I felt angry that he didn't understand what I was feeling. Dismissing my guilt didn't make it go away, it just made me feel like he wasn't listening to me. If he tried holding me, it felt like he was smothering me. If he gave me space, I felt like he was disappointed or annoyed with me for being so emotional, like he didn't want to be around me. Nothing he did was right, and I was desperately heartbroken, first that I couldn't seem to accept any of his attempts to help, and second, that he couldn't read my mind and figure out what would make me feel better. It was a hopelessly impossible situation. There was no answer, no "cure," no way out. The anger I would have at myself and at my life was volcanic. Sometimes it devolved into screaming into a pillow and pounding the mattress with my fists as I hid under the blankets on our bed. Other times it was slamming doors and kicking walls.

It was painful. It was agonizing. I hated hating myself. I hated showing so much weakness. I hated feeling so lost and so destroyed in my emotions that I could do nothing useful. I hated watching Jack do the dishes and the laundry because I couldn't bear to pry myself away from the safety of the couch to help.

Ironically, it was often in the darkest moments that I found my sanity again. Whatever was assailing me, whatever was trying to drag me down, would cause me to have horrible, frightening thoughts. Suddenly, I would realize that what I was thinking was not something that came from me. I would never have those thoughts on my own, I had no reason to. Jack was going to leave me, they would say. Or worse—I was going to leave Jack. As the attack progressed, the thoughts would get more and more destructive. I would never want those things, I would never do those things. And I would realize then that this wasn't me. These feelings weren't really mine. Yes, I was experiencing them and they were incredibly real, but they weren't mine. I could choose who I wanted to be. That didn't make it easy, and it didn't make it happen right away, but I could do it. I couldn't always choose how I felt, but I could choose how I wanted to feel, and that was a start. It was like falling to my death only to suddenly realize I had a parachute.

This realization, that sometimes my thoughts were not actually my own, helped me to picture what was happening to me. It was simple—I had a bully on my case. He took every opportunity he could to jab and push and hit, every little mistake, every tiny misunderstanding, every minor mishap was a chance for him to knock me off balance. He was excellent at attacking me when I was tired or on special days, like Christmas Eve or my birthday, when things were supposed to be wonderful and his attack would take me off guard the most. When the moment was right, he would strike hard and fast, and I would fall flat on my face. He would push me into a dark corner of my mind and do whatever it took to keep me there. He was ruthless and brutal and mean and hateful. Well, now that I knew he was there, I knew I could beat him. Sure, sometimes it meant getting pushed down over and over and over again before I finally was able to stand my ground, before I finally figured out his strategy and could form my own to counter it, but I knew what I was fighting, at least in a way. It was a step forwards, even if it was a small one.

We kept trying new things, Jack and I, new kinds of therapy. For my birthday a couple years after we got married, Jack got me a puppy—an adorable black lab, golden retriever mix that we named George. My wonderfully observant husband noticed how relaxed being around animals, especially dogs, made me, and on a bit of a whim he drove out to a farm that was practically giving away their mutt puppies and brought home George. He became my constant companion and an incredible support. I certainly credit him with much of the progress I was able to make. We didn't give him any special training other than the usual things, but somehow, innately, he always knew when I was hurting, and he would snuggle up to me as close as he could and listen to my tears. He would stay until he knew I was alright again, and then he would only leave to go get me one of his toys. "Here you go," he seemed to be saying. "This always makes me feel better. It squeaks."

I had dogs growing up, and they were always my best friends. Whenever anything went wrong, they always seemed to know and they always knew how to cheer me up. Humans don't always have such a strong intuition about those things. George, for me, did infinitely more than the psychologist and the pills ever could have.

Winter was tough, especially January and February. Going outside, going to the mountain, lying on the grass, listening to birds sing and leaves rustle, long days full of sunshine—these were things that helped, and they were entirely absent in wintertime. It was hard to find substitutions to compensate for their loss, so often these were my weaker months. I think George hated them as much as I did—you can only chase a ball so far in a tiny apartment, and besides me, I don't think there was anything he loved more than playing fetch.

The clouds would always pass, and once again I would be standing in the sunshine of life, living a peaceful, happy existence with my loving husband. Weeks, even months would go by before the darkness returned. I would hurt and ache and suffer and think it would never end. I would resign myself to the fact that every day of my life was going to be difficult, and every day of my life I would have to fight tooth and nail to be happy. But always, thanks to Jack and George and many others, there would be the sun again. And I would be a little stronger, a little more prepared for the next time. I recognized, not always right away, when my thoughts were my own and when some miserable, angry force was trying to plant its own thoughts and feelings in my head. It didn't make the feelings less strong or less poisonous, but it helped me keep my head through them. Sometimes I still screamed, sometimes I still pounded pillows or slammed doors, but gradually I was gaining control. I was learning how to fight back.

Sometimes, when I was feeling low for no apparent reason again, or when I would lose control of my emotions despite having carefully taken steps to avoid doing so, I would become desperately discouraged. I would feel unbelievably weak, and I would be angry that I knew what was happening and yet I still seemed unable or perhaps unwilling to stop it. In those moments, and they were many, Jack reassured me that I didn't get just one chance or one try at this. I got as many chances and tries as I would take.

Jack wasn't the perfect husband, and I wasn't the perfect wife. But each mistake brought the opportunity to grow stronger together as we worked through it. There was a lot of growth, much of it quite harrowing. Maybe the demon I was fighting truly was depression, or maybe it was something else. Either way, with every struggle I was increasing in my determination to overcome it. I knew that I wouldn't have my last battle until I drew my last breath, and maybe even then it wouldn't be over. But the times in between, those happy, peaceful times, were worth fighting for. Times like when we bought our first tent and were so excited that we attempted to camp in the mountains in April (we were home before it even got dark). Or, those summer nights when we would drive through the canyon to get to the other side of the mountain, away from the city, where we could see every star there was. Even those awful times when we both got sick at the same time and laid in bed groaning and whining until we couldn't stop laughing at how pathetic we were. Some of the best times, though, were our sunset walks out at the nature conservancy where we had our first date. I would fight to the death for moments like those.

My opposition never stopped trying to plant terrifying or devastating thoughts, and I would buy into them for a moment or two, but there was something I knew that made it possible for me to vanquish all such thoughts—I was loved. Jack loved me, I knew that. My family loved me. But most of all, as my mother had taught me every day that we were together, I knew that God loved me. With the most powerful being in the universe as my Heavenly Father, how could I ever be defeated? True, there were some days that certainly did not feel like a victory. But I picked myself up again. I tried again the next day. I kept going. Sometimes I failed, sometimes I triumphed. One step in front of the other, day in and day out.

For a long time I struggled with the concept so often taught in Christianity that struggle is good, suffering is good, trials are good.

Through all of my struggles thus far, yes, I suppose I came out the other side of them with more empathy for my fellow man, a little more understanding of others' shortcomings, maybe I could even say I came out a little stronger. But why was I being told I had to *enjoy* suffering? Finally it began to dawn on me that I was missing the point. Suffering is not fun. Duh, it's suffering. But with suffering comes many gifts. My character did improve, my relationship with God had a chance to deepen, and my capacity for joy expanded.

I once heard someone describe the Japanese art of kintsukuroi. She explained that it was the practice of taking a piece of broken pottery and repairing it using gold or silver. The result was stunning— far more so than the piece had been before it was broken. It was entirely unique, better and more beautiful for its trauma. Life couldn't be just an endless quest to find the next thing that would make me happy. Struggle was something to experience, not just endure or wait out. It wasn't just an accident or a glitch in the plan, it *was* the plan. It was what made the beautiful moments mean something. I learned that joy was something I had to choose and seek internally, not externally, no matter what else was happening to me. Maybe *that* was what Mom meant...peace and happiness can be yours whenever you want it enough. Did I want it enough to accept that God allows me to have trials in order to help me reach my potential?

The day we found out we were pregnant with our first child, my emotions spanned the entire spectrum. Elation, excitement, anticipation, instant love for the little person growing inside me— closely followed by alarm, fear, and dread. What if I broke in front of my child? What if they saw me fall apart? What if they thought it was their fault? What if they started to feel about themselves the way I sometimes felt about myself? What would I do on the days when getting out of bed felt like more than I could possibly accomplish? What if I was too wrapped up in my own despair to show them the love they deserved? What if, despite everything I was learning, I still failed? Still raged? Still doubted?

There was nothing I could do but wait and prepare.

Eight

Haley's light glowed bright and serene, despite the black smoke that engulfed the battalion. Like a lighthouse in the fog, she was steady, calm, and sure. The Darkness around her was heavy, like a thick blanket, but it had momentarily abandoned its siege on her consciousness.

Daniel, the demon, stood at the center of the wicked mist as it flowed in, low to the ground like black, scalding lava, oozing discontentedly towards its victim. Today, however, Daniel wasn't after Haley. Not directly at least. This high-ranking demon only occasionally accompanied his forces into battle. He prefered to direct and lead from a distance, waiting until the perfect moment when those he tortured were at their weakest and he could swoop in and finish the job. But today, his rancorous, boiling wrath and his seething glare were aimed at the battalion itself.

"Time and time again," he snarled. "So weak, so few, and yet time and time again you frustrate my designs. I have a plan for her!" he bellowed, his voice deranged with anger. From the end of his arm, a snake-like demon began to flow. It slithered slowly as it grew larger than a python. It had empty, black pits for eyes and monstrous, sharp fangs. "Suffocate them," commanded Daniel, his voice suddenly hollow. "Put out this vexing battalion. I will have no more of it."

Bent on the utter destruction of the guardians, the snake demon, followed by the Darkness and the rest of the swarm, attacked with ruthless, malicious intent. As usual, despair, anguish, and regret were their tools for this battle, but this time they were meant for the angels.

When she saw the darkness coming, Grace was ready and anxious to try out more of the wushu fighting technique she had been practicing. She took a deep breath and positioned her arms in a balletic hoop in front of her, one hand gripping her magnificent ribbon. She was surprised, however, when instead of trying to push past her, three of the demons, all of them the size of tigers, began circling her. Confused, she hesitated just a moment too long. Suddenly they pounced, and she was swept away in a barrage of memories.

For a moment, she was happy. She wore beautiful ballet slippers and a bouncy, lovely white tutu. She leapt and twirled and dipped and spun. She was the most graceful dancer in her class. The other girls frequently gasped at the beauty of her movement. She was humble, but her heart swelled with pride in her talent. She felt like she was floating, soaring even.

Then, one day, she felt a little more tired than usual. She

couldn't get her spins right, she felt too dizzy. She felt cold and weak. Her mom took her home and put her in bed, telling her she must have a cold or the flu and would need to rest. A day or two later, the nosebleeds started. Grace started noticing bruises on her skin. Then her bones started to hurt. The pounding headaches and the nausea soon followed.

In the car on the way home from the doctor, Grace watched her mom's face in the rear view mirror with acute anxiety. Why was she crying so much? Didn't she say it was just the flu? Grace had not liked it at all when the doctor took her blood, it made her head spin and her stomach churn.

"Momma?" she asked in a small, calm voice.

"Yes, Sweetheart?" her mom replied, her voice shaking through her tears.

"What's...leukemia?"

A few weeks later, it was the Spring recital for Grace's ballet class. She watched it from a wheelchair, her bald head covered in a beautiful pink scarf. Exhausted from all of the painful tests and treatments she had been subjected to constantly, she watched the recital with tears in her eyes that were both happy and sad. She was so proud of her classmates. Grace clutched her own ballet slippers in her arms, and wished with all her might that she could be up on stage with them. The tears never stopped, and her smile never faded.

"I want to dance," she whispered to her mom when it was all over. "Just for a minute. Do you think I could try?"

Her mom, who had also shed many tears, smiled and kissed her darling seven-year-old on the forehead.

"Maybe, Darling. Wait here."

She came back a few minutes later, and with eyes still gleaming, winked at Grace.

When everyone else had gone, and all her classmates had come to her to say how much they missed her and wished she could come back to class, the old man that ran the little theater turned the music and the lights back on. Grace's mother gingerly lifted her out of her wheelchair and carried her to the stage, where together they floated and soared. One arm clutched tightly around her mother's neck, the other outstretched, Grace danced her last dance.

Dima, who was awaiting the onslaught, saw Grace collapse to her knees, her hands on the ground in front of her face, barely able to support her. Only one of the large demons remained, the prey sufficiently weakened that it could handle her on its own. Its great, gnarled paws were on her back, forcing her down. Dima instantly started towards her, a katana raised and ready to strike the Darkness that oppressed his friend and fellow guardian. However, before he had taken more than a few steps, he was overtaken by a huge swell of the black fog. Like a giant ocean wave, it collided with him and he, too, was swept away into his darkest memories.

He and his best friend were pinned down in the middle of Stalingrad in a large hole left by a Luftwaffe air attack. The battle had been raging on for what must have been weeks. The Russian army, Dima's army, was finally making progress against the onslaught of Nazi troops. Somehow, however, he found himself wholly stuck. An entire squad of Nazi soldiers was coming their way.

"Sasha, we're in big trouble," Dima said to his childhood

friend. He laughed a little, the kind of laugh you give when so much has gone wrong. That morning, Dima had woken up with a lightness in his heart, a feeling like it was going to be a wonderful day. Something good was going to happen, he was sure, but as the hours passed, one thing after another had gone wrong. An unexpected move from the Germans, a bad call by an officer, ammunition shortages, an accident with the day's rations that left everyone hungry, one thing after another, and now this.

Sasha, however, did not laugh. He looked terrified. His eyes darted in every direction, he was hyperventilating, and his hands clutched his gun so tightly it looked like he might crush the thing. Dima saw Sasha's distress and put a hand on his shoulder, changing his grin from humoured to encouraging.

"It's okay, my friend. We're going to be okay! Here's what we're going to do. I'll cover you while you run to that building, and from there, you can cover me while I run to join you. It's easy. It will only take a few seconds, and then we can meet up with the Lieutenant and the rest."

Sasha nodded rapidly.

"Okay," he said between quick, shallow breaths, his face contorted with fear. "Okay."

Dima smiled and straightened his friend's helmet. He put his back to the wall of the hole and slowly, carefully, peered over its edge. He quickly pulled himself back to the bottom of the hole, his face betraying a new concern.

"Alright. There are a few more of them than we thought, Sasha. They are coming this way, but I don't think they know we're here. The surprise will give us just enough time. We are going to have to do this faster than we've ever done anything in our lives, alright?"

Sasha nodded rapidly again.

"Alright. On my count. One...two...THREE!"

Dima flung himself over the edge of the hole so that his head, shoulders, arms, and gun were vulnerable. He let loose as many shots as he could into the advancing German troops. The surprise worked, and they scrambled to find the source of the attack just long enough for Sasha to make his escape. Dima cheered for his friend, then readied himself to follow. He waited for Sasha's cover fire. The shots never came. He looked towards the building that had sheltered his friend in time to see the last of him running around the corner. Sasha abandoned Dima.

He could hear the Nazis' boots scraping on the ground, kicking debris as they went. He could hear their shouts, hear them rushing around, trying to find him. It wouldn't take long, he knew. His mind raced, unable to comprehend the fact that Sasha had left him for dead. Sasha, who had been as good as a brother to him since his earliest memories. Sasha, who had fallen in love with and intended to marry Dima's sister as soon as the war was over. Sasha, who had told that sister—Dima's only remaining family—that they would come home to her together.

He thought of the fear he had seen in Sasha's eyes, and he felt angry and sad. His heart jumped around in his chest so hard he half expected it to break through his uniform. The clip on the strap that went around his neck, holding his gun close to him, clattered as his hands trembled. He closed his eyes tight, and held his breath. How could this be happening? A moment ago, it was alright. It was almost an adventure. His best friend was at his side. Now he was alone. He would die alone, abandoned by a brother.

David saw Grace and Dima go down, one after the other. He felt a surge of something...fear? It raced through his spirit, from head to foot—the strongest echo he had felt yet. He raised his cane to bring it down and send a charge of light out to his friends, but before he could finish the motion, a ferocious flock of winged demons, each barely smaller than the man himself, rushed in and overcame him. They swallowed him up in a haunting memory.

Images swam before his eyes. A hospital room, a bouquet of flowers on the windowsill, his wife...his dear, sweet wife…

The surgery had been a success, but David's old body was not healing like it should have. The doctors didn't know what to say, except that sometimes this happens with the elderly.

"But you said it worked, the surgery worked," his wife, Janey, insisted to Dr. Rose. Dr. Rose inhaled deeply, nodding.

"It did. But that's not the problem anymore, Mrs. Emerson. The problem is that David's body is too weak to heal itself. Remember, we talked about this before we ever agreed to the procedure?" He was trying to be gentle, but he didn't know what else to tell the small, white-haired woman. It had been a routine procedure, and he had carefully explained the risks of any kind of surgery on such an old body.

"So what do we do now?" Janey demanded, her small fists balled up and her eyes wide.

"Sweetheart, sit down, please," David asked from his hospital bed. He was worried that a panic attack would hit Janey, like they often did, and put her in a bed next to him. His head felt foggy, and even just speaking seemed to drain him of the little energy he had left in his frail, failing body.

"No! No, they have to fix this!" she insisted, her voice rising and becoming shrill. "*You* have to fix this!" she almost screamed, jamming her finger at Dr. Rose.

"Mrs. Emerson, there's just nothing we can do…" Dr Rose tried to explain.

"Nonsense! You're a doctor, of course there's something you can do!" Janey yelled, waving her hand at David to hush his continued pleas for her to sit down. Dr. Rose nodded.

"Yes, you're right. We can make him comfortable, and hope for the best."

Janey's rage silenced her, and while she fumbled for words, David nodded to Dr. Rose, allowing him to excuse himself.

"Darling, please," David begged weakly. "Please, come sit by me. I want to hold your hand, Love, please."

Still fuming, and after giving a stomp of her small foot, Janey huffed over to the chair next to David's bed and sat down brusquely.

"Make you comfortable? Can you believe it?" she seethed. David reached for her hand, but she was too busy glaring at the door where the doctor had exited to see it.

"My dear, don't you remember that we discussed this before? I'm not a young man anymore, my body is tired. It was a risk we had to take. Remember? Darling, at this age, there isn't much time left anyway. Wouldn't you rather we have some time together now, than be surprised later by an aneurysm or a heart attack?" David's heart was breaking. He wasn't afraid to die, but he knew Janey was terrified to be alone. He reached for her hand again, and this time she gave it to him.

"No, this is outrageous. This should not be happening. You should be coming home with me tomorrow." Janey's furious tone began betraying her grief. Her voice cracked and her lip trembled as she spoke.

"Maybe I will! I've licked ailments before, Beautiful. No one said death was certain, not just yet," he said, trying to be cheerful. His head spun, so he pinched his eyes shut. Janey wrenched her hand away and stood up so fast, she stumbled.

"Stop! Just stop it! How can you sit there and smile when you are leaving me? You're leaving me, David! You're going, that's what he said! He said they can make you comfortable—"

"And hope for the best," David interjected. Janey glared at him.

"That's what they say when they can't bring themselves to tell you there *is* no hope," she snapped.

David felt weary. He let himself sink a little further into his pillows and closed his eyes again. They were doing a good job, keeping him comfortable. He felt less pain than he had in the better part of a decade. They never fought, he and Janey. But she was scared, and that made her angry. He knew she was worried about everything— the house, the yard, the bills, the dog. David had taken care of it. He wished now he had time to explain it all to her. But, he thought, the kids will do that. The kids will take care of her just fine. Her trepidation was more about loneliness than bills.

He could hear her walk to the chair and collapse into it. She began weeping. She was terrified of being left behind. The thought made her feel like her lungs were constricting and her heart was pounding on her ribs. David opened his eyes, from which tears were streaming. How could he go now? How could he leave Janey like this?

Having formed their usual circle around Haley, Eden had her back to most of the battalion and didn't notice anything was wrong as she braced herself for the attack until, out of the corner of her eye, she saw David collapse. His face was contorted in what looked like grief, and half a dozen bird demons were circling him tightly. Surprised, it took Eden a moment to react. Of course, demons always attacked the guardians. What was strange, however, was the focus with which they were doing it—not one of them was making any move for Haley. As Eden moved to pull back her slingshot to fire on David's oppressor, however, the black snake was suddenly inches from her face and it's long body wrapped around her own. It constricted before she could even cry out, and now she stared her past in the face like the others.

It was a cold November night. Not quite freezing, but cold enough to see your breath clearly. The alleyway was quiet, but for the *drip drip drip* of the rainwater still making its way down the rooftops and off the gutters, though the storm had passed hours before. Empty clotheslines, which had been hastily cleared that afternoon, were beaded with moisture.

Shouts came from one of the apartments.

"You get back here, you useless, ugly brat!" raged a man.

"No! You stay away from me, you murderer!" screamed a young girl.

"Get over here! I am going to teach you some respect!"

"You touch me and I'll kill you! I swear I'll kill you!"

There was a crash and a furious, pained yell from the man. Then the sharp *snap* of a slamming door. Then there was pounding on the door, like someone was trying to break through the wood. Now there was a light coming from the window, and someone was scrambling with the lock.

All at once, a young, redheaded girl flew out of the window and onto the fire escape, closely followed by the reaching hand of what appeared to be a very large man. Up against the railing of the fire escape, she was just out of his reach, and he was too big to come out after her. Careful not to get too close, she made her way to the ladder, pulled the latch and let it down.

"You stupid brat, get back here!"

"Nope," she said, all of the sudden carefree. "I don't think I will."

She was wearing a ballcap and overalls over a tattered, long-sleeved shirt that was much too big for her. The cold snaked its way through the thin fabric and pricked her skin, but she ignored it, pretending like it was the perfect night to be outside. Her auburn hair was cut short and framed her face, making her steely blue eyes stand out against the dark night as she glared at the man.

"You good-for-nothing little demon, you better not show your face here ever again!"

"Don't intend to," she said blithely as she climbed down the ladder.

"You're stupid and worthless, just like your mother!"

Eden paused her descent for a moment, then, taking a couple

steps back up, poked her head through the hole in the platform of the fire escape.

"Mama wasn't stupid or worthless. You murdered her. You made her so sad, it killed her. *You're* the one that's stupid, cause now you're all alone. I hope it kills you, too."

With that, she left behind a sad, abusive life to make her own way on the streets of New York.

For a few weeks, she did well by doing odd jobs for women she could convince to pay her. She carried groceries, swept porches, even did laundry and scrubbed dishes. After a while, though, the women didn't have so many chores to help with, or at least they said they didn't. Sometimes they would still give her a crust of bread or some scraps from the kitchen. One particularly kind woman tearfully gave her a coat. It had clearly belonged to a little boy, but Eden didn't mind. It was warm. And from the sad look on the woman's face, that little boy wouldn't be needing it anymore.

She thought herself a right success at living on the streets. She made friends with some of the other urchins, and sometimes they let her sleep next to them to help keep each other warm. The winter came on hard, though, and when the snow hit, her feet, covered only by the socks she had on when she escaped, froze. Barely able to walk, she could do nothing but beg for food, and she was too proud to do that. She found a corner in an alley that was protected from the wind and most of the snow and made it her new home.

There was a little girl, a few years younger than she was, that also lived on the streets, who had taken a liking to Eden. Every now and then she brought her some food, but as the winter deepened and darkened, she came to Eden's corner less and less.

Eden, fierce in her desolation, was glad to be where she was. *Better die here than in that dump of a home*, she thought. With every breath, she felt her lungs turn to ice. After a while, though, the pain faded, and so did she.

Stephanie felt it coming for her. Her eyes were closed gently, as they always were just before a fight, and she knew this time was going to be different. This time, they didn't want Haley. She didn't fight when the Darkness reached her and pulled her into a hateful, smothering embrace and the thoughts and images she had finally moved past started playing again in her mind.

She didn't remember how it happened. She and her two best friends were driving home one night, and somehow the driver lost control of the car. It went into the shoulder and slid sideways into the guardrail, which came through the car right where Stephanie was sitting. She had dozed off before it happened, so the last thing she remembered was laughing with her friends at something ridiculous one of them had said.

The next thing she knew, she was standing next to her own hospital bed, invisible to everyone else in the room. Her parents stayed by her side, and her younger siblings were there as regularly as they could be. She had sustained a terrible head injury, broken ribs, broken collar bone, a collapsed lung, and many other lesser injuries. She watched their tears, she listened to their prayers, she heard their grief and frustration, and she witnessed their great bravery and love as day by day passed, and all she could do, caught between life and death, was watch and wait.

Ten long days went by, and soon the doctors' initial hopefulness wore off and turned to regret and heartfelt sympathy. It was time to let her go. Stephanie didn't want to go—she wanted to stay, to wake up, to hold her siblings and be held by her parents. She didn't want to see them cry anymore, she didn't want to cause them more anguish than they had already gone through. Yet, as she eavesdropped on the doctors, she knew it was time. Something was pulling her elsewhere, some sense of excitement and adventure, like someone, somewhere, was impatiently waiting for her to say her goodbyes.

Although she knew they couldn't feel it, she kissed each one of her three brothers and two sisters as they gathered around her bed for their final farewell. She tried ruffling the youngest brother's hair, but with no effect. With a heavy sigh and a crooked smile—as if ruffling it could make it any messier anyway—she turned to look at her parents. She knew their hearts were shattering. She knew their devastation was intense and would take many years to ease. But she knew they were strong. They were brave and kind. She kissed her father, then her mother. With one arm around each of them, she held them tight. She wished they knew she was there.

"I love you Mama, Papa. I'll be here, for all of you, until you don't hurt so much anymore. Then I'll still check on you often. Don't cry, Mama. Something wonderful is waiting for me. Oh, Papa, please don't be sad for me. I'll be waiting for you, for all of you. I love you."

"I love you, Steph," whispered her father.

"I love you, baby girl," wept her mother.

The doctor turned off the life support machines.

Henry stood next to Haley like he usually did. He was in awe of her light. It hadn't shined that bright and that strong since she was a little child. Oh, how she had shined then. Almost like she had before she came to this life. He was so proud, so relieved. He knew it was temporary, that eventually she would feel low again, dim again, but in that moment he couldn't be happier. Now she knew, as well as he did, that there was hope. So much of her life lately had been a struggle, so many of her joys had been clawed to pieces by doubts, fears, anxiety, grief. He could sense the peace in her. She was just throwing the ball for George at their favorite park, but he knew that she was experiencing a clarity and a lightness that was almost forgotten to her. In that moment, she felt worth. In that moment, she was whole.

Darkness licked at Henry's heels. It was struggling to get close to him, due to his proximity to Haley's brilliance. Daniel watched nearby, viciously commanding his strongest demons forward, despite their pained hisses. Crawling on their bellies, they grasped at his ankles, sinking their toxic, despair-laced claws into his spirit. As Henry watched Haley, flashes of his past stole into his consciousness. A beautiful, well-built cabin. His stunning wife, pregnant with their first child. A swing hanging from a tree in front of the cabin, waiting to fly. Perturbed, Henry swiped at the darkness with his hand, but the snake demon seized him and started climbing up his arm. His wife's face contorted with terrifying pain, covered in sweat and tears. A brand new baby, only moments old, not crying, not moving. His little chest barely rising and falling. A tiny coffin, a vacant stare in his wife's eyes. Blood on the straw mattress...so much blood.

With that, he was wrenched into the full memory. The demons, their hold finally secure, threw him to the ground and pressed him to it, clawing and biting. Daniel sneered contentedly, relishing the moment. Henry remembered that tiny little boy, his perfect little body. Why hadn't he lived? Henry couldn't understand. What had happened? And Beth...his sweet, beautiful, charming Beth...the bleeding never stopped. In her grief, she had little will to fight for her own life. She laid there for three days, staring into nothingness, silent tears always present in her eyes.

In one moment of lucidity, she had finally spoken to Henry. She reached up and touched his face as he carefully wiped her brow with a cool towel.

"My darling Henry," she said faintly. "My love, I want to be with you, always…"

Henry kissed her forehead.

"You will be, always."

A tear fell as she pinched her eyes shut and smiled a sad, regretful smile.

"I have to go...our baby...he needs me…"

Henry's heart sank dramatically.

"No, Beth, no—"

She put her hand over his mouth tenderly, and when she was sure he wouldn't speak more, she let it drop and closed her eyes.

The next morning, she was gone. He buried them together, near the tree that held the lonely swing.

Henry had spent many years alone. Beth had been an unexpected joy in his quiet, solitary life. For reasons he could not explain, she loved him more deeply than anyone had since his parents.

She found him clever and talented, and he doted on her every moment he was with her. The quiet and the aloneness returned when she died, but it wasn't as peaceful as it had once been. Now it was emptiness, blackness, nothingness.

Several tortuous years passed, and nothing changed. He went into town when he had to, he did odd jobs when his supplies ran out. Otherwise, he stayed in his mountain, in his cabin. One winter, he came down with tuberculosis. He was too stubborn to go into town for help until it was too late and he was too weak to travel. Burning with fever, coughing violently, he slowly deteriorated until he knew the end was near. *Good,* he thought. *There is nothing for me here. I am nothing here.*

Every member of the battalion was on their knees. The Darkness, in all its forms, became shadows of Daniel, all shaped like him, all with a knee pressed into the backs of the guardians, each of whom could do nothing as they were forced to their lowest. A tear dropped from Henry's eye, but made no mark where it fell. He heard a quiet *tsk tsk* in his ear. Struggling against the pressure pushing him down, he lifted his head to see Daniel crouching down next to him, arm draped over his knee as he leaned over to look Henry in the eye.

"Why so sad, Captain?" the demon hissed. His black eyes glinted with pleasure and his lips were curled in a wicked smile.

"You," Henry breathed with some difficulty.

"Me!" exclaimed his oppressor delightedly. "Yes, me. Never will you be rid of me, dear, sweet, friend."

Henry could feel the dark creature's malice sinking into him like sharp, murderous teeth. He felt the searing hatred, the blinding

bitterness, and the wild animosity shoot through him like venom.
It coursed through his spirit quickly and mercilessly. Again and
again, the agony of his loss attacked him ferociously. He felt like he
couldn't breath, he couldn't see, he couldn't think, he couldn't feel
anything else but pain—immense, soul-crushing agony. He could
hear the demon laughing now, cackling as he watched his prey suffer,
eerily echoed by his vile clones. Henry wished there was some kind
of second death, something that would deliver him from the hellish
nightmare in which he was now trapped. There was no hope, there was
no light, there was nothing but darkness.

Then, for a moment, Henry was reminded of his battalion. He
knew they must be suffering just as he was. He knew they had their
own demons driving them down as low as they could. He was sure
they were fighting, he was certain they were enduring. That thought
allowed for another one to battle its way into his conscience...Beth.
She wasn't gone. She wasn't lost. And Benjamin...he was able to see
them almost anytime he wanted, and when the war was finally over,
they would be together forever. Nothing, absolutely nothing, could
keep that from happening.

In the back of his mind, Henry heard his demon let out an
animal-like growl.

"What are you doing here?"

Henry felt warmth wash over him. He felt strength return to his
limbs, sense return to his mind, life return to his soul. A hand rested
on his shoulder, and his whole being seemed to explode with light.
He grasped the hand. He could feel the scar in its center. And then the
voice...that sweet, gentle, yet thundering and piercing voice that he had

heard when he first left his mortal life…

"Peace be unto you."

The darkness was dispelled, wholly, perfectly, absolutely.

Nine

Being pregnant is a difficult thing to anticipate. People explain what it's like, share their experiences, and assure you it'll be the same for you, but until you have another human being swimming around your insides, I don't think anyone really knows what to expect.

It took a month or two, maybe even three, for me to believe it. Oh, I was definitely not feeling normal. Something was up, that was for sure, but pregnant? What does that even mean? I was so tired during my first trimester. I could barely peel myself up off the couch once or twice a day to feed myself or let George out. Poor dog, I'm surprised he didn't actually die of boredom. I have never felt so exhausted, so entirely depleted. And so hungry! I was always hungry—famished! But, nothing sounded appetizing. Jack would suggest one thing after another, and I would grimace and grumpily demand to know why he was trying to make me throw up, and then why he was letting me starve.

By the time winter started to fade and my belly started to really grow, things shaped up. I could feel my baby moving inside of me, sometimes I could even see an elbow or a knee or maybe his head press out against my tummy. I could eat anything and everything. I had my energy back, and I was loving this human-making stuff. It still didn't seem very real, not until we started receiving gifts and buying things to prepare for our little one's arrival. Holding those tiny clothes up, and realizing there would soon be a tiny person wearing them... well, it was surreal. *Too* real. How could I possibly be a parent? Jack, I could see—he was patient, calm, strong, all those things you need to be. Me, on the other hand...I was emotional, anxious, and scared. Not exactly the best tools to have in your parental belt.

Although I felt good emotionally during the pregnancy, there were still a few times that the negative feelings came on so strongly, I felt sure I was already traumatizing my unborn child. How could he not be feeling what I was feeling, at least to some degree? Whether he was or not, it suddenly became clear to me that I could not afford to be anything other than my best self. It wasn't just me and Jack that would be dealing with this anymore— this little person, this perfect, wonderful, beautiful little person would be thrown right into the middle of whatever kind of emotional and spiritual life we provided. I wanted it to be the best it could be. I was learning to give up perfection, but it at least had to be good.

So, I did something I swore I'd never do again. I met with a therapist. This time it was one that *I* chose, with Jack's help. She was wonderful, and I realized that maybe I had slammed the door on that kind of support a little too finally and a little too hastily before. To be fair, the first time really was bad.

Meeting with her didn't magically make everything better, but she helped me get to know myself a little more, and knowing myself taught me compassion for myself, which was something I had been sorely lacking. I finally was able to acknowledge parts of me that I had always thought of as parasitic outsiders trying to attack me and suck the joy out of my life—things I had to fight, I had to destroy, in order to be whole. But when I actually took a moment to look inside myself, to find in my mind's eye where the hurt was coming from, I didn't see the raging monster I expected. Instead, I stumbled upon parts of my soul that were so beat up, so shunned and snuffed and abused—by me—that I wanted to weep for them. Those parts of me, though I was still working out exactly what they were, had important, wonderful things to teach me, things they wanted, out of kindness and love, to give me. Unfortunately, I had lumped them in with my demons and so was fighting on both sides of this internal battle.

It was all quite novel, and it took a lot of time to wrap my head around it, but this new therapy, coupled with the other things I was doing to combat my Darknesses, seemed to at least level the playing field. I wasn't so helplessly bullied into that corner anymore, and if it did come to that, I could come back out swinging. It was a difficult lesson to learn that even with all the right tools and knowledge, there would still be a lot of extremely low days, or at least hours. It dawned on me that there would *never* be a point in my life when strife and struggle and pain were behind me for good. Those things would always be part of my existence. They were supposed to be. Without the cracks and the breaks, there was no room for the gold and the silver. Knowing how to live a beautiful life not in spite of, but perhaps even because of my challenges and trials became my new goal. That, and survive childbirth.

My due date came ever nearer. My belly button popped right out. We got the nursery set up, we had a list of names to choose from, I made several meals and put them in the freezer, Jack packed the hospital bag two months in advance, we were *ready*!

Then the due date came and went, and still no baby. Two days, three days, four...although my anxiety at being a parent was coming to an all time high, I was ready to have him in my arms. Mom had said in her list that she loved me before I was even born, that she waited for me with great joy and longing. I had come, over the months, to understand that love. I desperately hoped I wasn't going to mess this kid up for life, but I was ready to give him the best of me, to try.

Finally, my doctor decided we'd better induce labor. We went to the hospital and they put the blasted IV in (I later insisted that was the worst part of the whole experience, which Jack emphatically denied), and started the medications that would bring my baby to the outside world.

The room we were in was nice. I'd always hoped to have a natural birth, preferably at home. I liked the sound of curling up in my own bed, being in my own space, after such an ordeal as childbirth. Jack, on the other hand, was extremely wary of such things. So, I agreed that we would have our first in the hospital, just to see how my body handles labor and delivery, and then we could revisit the topic with our second baby. I pictured a stark, ugly, cold room with a rock hard bed and mean nurses. To my delight, it was quite the opposite. Our room was spacious and had windows all the way across one wall that looked out on beautiful trees. It was a fortunate view—one more room to the left or right, and we would have been staring at the parking lot. The nurses were all incredibly kind and patient, and the bed was admittedly small, but very comfortable. We settled in and waited for something exciting to happen.

Hours ticked by, one at a time, and there was very little change, almost no progress. I wasn't sure what to think or how to feel...was everything okay? A full twelve hours passed and I had only dilated about two centimeters. When my water broke a couple hours later, things started to get intense really fast. Everyone tells you childbirth is the worst pain there is, and while I've never really had to experience any other kind of intense physical pain, I can tell you it was no walk in the park. My body felt like it was being torn apart. Everything I'd read or heard about giving birth naturally said to just "relax and embrace the pain," and it won't be so bad. I got it, that was an idea I was working with emotionally, so why not implement it physically? Had someone tried to tell me to just relax and embrace the pain at that point, though, I might have punched them in the face. Obviously I still had some work to do on that particular concept.

I kept at it, though, until a few hours later when the doctor said I was only dilated to about 3 centimeters. I was done with the whole "natural birth" thing. I was given, or may have demanded, an epidural. At last the endless succession of agonizing contractions became nothing more than spikes on the monitor next to my bed. As I finally relaxed and listened to my baby's heart pound away on yet another machine I was hooked to, I thought there must be another metaphor in there somewhere...we don't have to fight all our battles, especially our worst ones, alone, right? I drifted off before I could think too much about it.

The sweet sleep that came next lasted what felt like just moments before the nightmares started. The same face showed up in each of them—a face that would have been handsome but for the wicked glint in his eye and the cruel grin distorting his mouth. He wore a sleek, black suit and he was tall and slender. Over and over again, for one reason or another, he said he was there to take my baby.

"You aren't fit to be a mother," he said in a quiet, penetrating voice. "You aren't stable. You aren't capable. You aren't ready. You aren't...you aren't...you aren't..."

In the bewildering dreamstate I was in, I couldn't move fast enough, I couldn't speak clearly enough, I couldn't stop him from taking my baby away from me. In my dream he was already born, lying in a bassinet nearby. Over and over again, I watched the man in black take my little one out of his bed and walk out the door of my hospital room with him, while I scrambled to control my body and my mind to chase after him.

Never had I felt so helpless, so desperate. I was screaming, I was weeping, I was raging, I was sure I was dying. I wrenched the IV out of my arm, I swung my legs over the edge of my bed and immediately collapsed to the floor. No longer was it the sunny, peaceful place we had come to. The floor was metallic and cold, the room was dark and ugly. Crawling across the floor towards that door, because I couldn't balance myself enough to stand, even to get up on my knees, I knew I would never stop until my baby was back in my arms.

"Give him back!" I sobbed. "He's *my* baby!"

I was vaguely aware of other noises around me.

"She won't wake up?" said one concerned voice.

"No! She was so tired, I just thought she was sleeping, but I can't get her to respond at all," came another voice, this one familiar... so familiar.

There was beeping, clanging, rapid talking. I felt jostled and pinched and pushed, but I didn't have time for that, I had to get my baby! I fought against all of the influences bearing down on me, I fought through my unbalance, I pressed on towards that door. That man, whoever he was, had my baby. Maybe I wasn't stable. Maybe I wasn't ready or capable, but I was his mother, and I was trying, and no one would stop me from protecting him. I had been through so many battles for my mind and my heart, I knew how to fight and I wouldn't stop now! I clawed my way across the floor, inch by inch.

"What's happening? Someone please tell me what's going on!"

"I know you're concerned, we're doing everything we can, Jack. Please, stay out of our way so we can help her."

That awful, sickly sweet voice was in my ear again.

"Don't try, Haley. You're embarrassing yourself. There's nothing left for you. You will never be worth anything. You're fooling yourself. You will never be able to raise a child, you can barely take care of yourself. Just give up. Just stop trying. Just lie down and stay down."

I felt the last of my strength draining from my body, I could barely drag myself another inch. My weeping was uncontrollable. He was right. I was worthless. I couldn't do anything right. Everything I thought I learned suddenly seemed so ridiculous. Who was I to think I could be a mother? Who was I kidding? My despair was screaming through me like a jagged, endless bolt of hot, destroying lightening.

Then, I felt a gentle, firm hand on my shoulder. Tears still flooding from my eyes, I turned to see who it was. Crouching next to me, holding what looked like a sword on fire, was a middle-aged man. He was so familiar, yet through my tears I couldn't make out his features clearly. He didn't seem as solid as a regular person, he was faint around the edges, but his eyes stood out in their fierceness. His gaze was on the door, just a few feet from my fingertips. There was another hand on my other shoulder. I turned again and this time saw a beautiful, red-haired young girl. She wore a baseball cap backwards, and she, too, had a fierceness about her. Unlike the hostility that I felt from the man in black, however, I sensed great warmth and love from these two newcomers.

"We're here, Haley," said the man, looking at me for the first time. He smiled, and I felt overwhelmed with relief. I wasn't alone.

"We're all here," said the girl, gesturing over her shoulder. I pulled myself up on my elbows and saw a whole group of people standing behind me. There was a young man holding a battle ax, and a small girl practically bouncing up and down on her tip-toes, whipping a golden ribbon around. There was an old man with a glowing cane, and a young woman I was sure I knew from somewhere that emanated holy light. Next to her was another familiar face, though she seemed younger, healthier than I remembered...Mom? And next to her was a big black dog that I knew at once. They seemed to be waiting on some command.

"She can see us! She can see us!" squealed the small girl with the ribbon. The older man, smiling, put his hand on her shoulder.

"Steady, Grace, steady."

The man next to me stood. He reached down to me with his hand. I looked at it, but was so sure that I didn't have the strength to take it.

"Nothing you have been through is for nothing. You are stronger because of your struggle. We need you, Haley. This is your fight. This is your life."

I looked around at the small army.

"Who are you?" I asked. They all seemed so familiar. The old man's voice...I had heard it before. And the redhead, I recognized her voice, too! The porch...the morning of the funeral...

"Get up, Haley," said the man with the sword, reaching even further for me. Determination swelled in my chest. I would never, ever give up. Never. I grabbed his hand.

The second my skin touched his, I suddenly woke up with a gasp and a start. I was surrounded by doctors and nurses, all with worried expressions and speaking quietly and nervously to each other. Upon my return to consciousness, they froze and stared at me. After a moment, the busy activity resumed.

"Vitals are normalizing. Everything looks good!"

"Okay, Haley, you're right on time—it's time to push, do you think you can push?"

A few difficult minutes later, a tiny wail filled the air, and my heart exploded with a joy that was at once painful and brilliant. A few moments more and he was there in my arms. No one was going to take him from me. No one was going to tell me I couldn't be his mother. No one was going to tell me I couldn't be anything anymore. Jack was by my side, tears racing down his face in relief and delight. He kissed my face over and over again.

"I thought I was going to lose both of you," he wept. I kissed him.

"Don't you worry, Daddy," I said, gazing into the face of my perfect, beautiful baby. "Everything is going to be just fine. Isn't that right, Henry?"

At the sound of his name, the tiny bundle in my arms opened his eyes and looked at us for the first time. Finally, we were together.

Epilogue

Eden stood on one side of the bassinet, Henry stood on the other. The nursery was full of sleeping newborns and guardian angels. It was a bright, golden place. Eden's eyes were wide as she stared into the little face in front of her. Still as a statue, she was afraid to move lest she wake him. Henry looked down at the babe and smiled. He loved meeting souls fresh from heaven.

Eden shifted her weight, and the marbles in her pouch jingled. The baby before her stirred and opened his eyes. He blinked and squinted for a few seconds, then his gaze settled on Eden. She gasped and froze.

"He's looking right at me!" she said in an alarmed whisper. Henry nodded.

"He'll be able to see us for a few weeks, maybe months. Being born is quite the ordeal, this way we can ease him into it. We're sort of like an echo for him—a reminder of heaven, a reminder that he's special and never alone."

Eden's eyes grew wider the longer the tiny infant looked at her.

"Why is he staring at me?" she asked in wonder, still frozen in place.

"Because he knows you," Henry said with a warm grin.

"What?" Eden breathed, incredulous. "How?"

Eden was usually headstrong and even a little rowdy. She swaggered, she joked, she didn't hesitate to swing a playful punch. But now, she was stunned into reverence and stillness.

"Well," said Henry, inhaling deeply, "you're already friends. You're the captain of his Battalion, Eden."

The strongest echo she had yet felt jolted through her body like a surge of electricity. It zinged her, from head to toe, perhaps a feeling stronger than she had felt even with her physical body. Excitement, trepidation, shock.

"Me?" she stammered.

"You."

"You are here to be loved and to give love to those around you, and nothing else really matters—it's that simple."

www.ingramcontent.com/pod-product-compliance
Lightning Source LLC
Chambersburg PA
CBHW072032170626
46811CB00008B/3049